Starflight to Eternity

Books by Patrick Dearen

Grizzly Moon
The End of Nowhere
Haunted Border
Apache Lament
Dead Man's Boot
The Big Drift
Starflight to Destiny
To Hell or the Pecos
Perseverance
When the Sky Rained Dust
The Hidden Treasure of the Chisos
On the Pecos Trail
Comanche Peace Pipe
When Cowboys Die
The Illegal Man
Starflight to Eternity (a.k.a. Starflight to Faroul)

Nonfiction
Bitter Waters: The Struggles of the Pecos River
Devils River: Treacherous Twin to the Pecos, 1535-1900
Lone Star Lost
Saddling Up Anyway: The Dangerous Lives of Old-Time Cowboys
Halff of Texas
The Last of the Old-Time Cowboys
A Cowboy of the Pecos
Crossing Rio Pecos
Portraits of the Pecos Frontier
Castle Gap and the Pecos Frontier, Revisited

Starflight to Eternity

Patrick Dearen

SPEAKING VOLUMES, LLC
NAPLES, FLORIDA
2023

Starflight to Eternity
(a.k.a. Starflight to Faroul)

Copyright © 1980, 2013 by Patrick Dearen

All rights reserved. No part of this book may be reproduced or
transmitted in any form or by any means without written permission.

ISBN 979-8-89022-010-3

To my father, Delbert Dearen (1912-1998)
and to my grandmother, Lucy B. Dearen (1890-1984)

Chapter One

"Faroul. I was there. I touched it. I held the secret of creation in my hands. It was mine, but I lost it. I lost it, and I can never have it again!"

Alan Burke lay in the dark with his head pressed into the filthy floor and listened as rats scurried through cracks in the rock wall. It was cold, and the breath that came in spurts from his nostrils felt warm against his gnarled hand. When he stretched out his leg the joints were stiff and the muscles did not want to respond, as if he supported a great load.

Yes, he said to himself, remembering for the thousandth time the old man's haunting words. *Faroul, the power of life, is out there somewhere. It's out there, but I can never have it either.*

No, it had been too long. He had been trapped here in the dungeons and mines of the penal colony, Alos, for too many years, too many eons. His hair had turned too gray, his muscles too lax. And worst of all, his willpower had diminished like sap wrenched from a once-powerful oak. He knew he would live and die here with only the rats and his own decaying heartbeat to keep him company, all because he had trusted, only to be betrayed.

Betrayed! The memory sent a chill through his spine and left his blood coursing through his veins like a rampaging river.

He sucked in the air that reeked with his own urine and slammed his fist into the floor. Betrayed! No! Poteet would not get away with it. Somehow, some way, he would get out of here and sink his fingers into Poteet's swarthy neck until his breaths were a gasp and his face pale as a sun through a morning fog.

Anger swelled inside him like a cancer: anger at Poteet, at himself, even at the old man Kasterfayette for ever filling his mind with visions of Faroul. Why couldn't he lie here in solitude and die? Why did he have to listen without end to the esoteric words that never would give him peace?

Damn him! Damn Faroul! Why couldn't the memories just leave him alone?

Alan suddenly felt a great tremor pass through him, jerking spasmodically at his chest like an electrical shock. Abruptly, it was as if he were aware of things, events, of which he should have had no conception.

He raised himself to his elbow and whirled. What was it that made him feel this way, that gave him the sensation he was an observer outside life's progression of events, watching and biding his time?

It wasn't the darkness, thick and swirling as always, or the odor of dingy sleeping furs in the corner, or the rats that played along his tattered pants leg. It was not even his own heart knocking against his rib cage like the thud of an animal's hooves.

No, it was something different . . . alien, mysterious, powerful.

He dragged himself across the floor, his legs deadened like slabs of meat. He stopped, finding a thin shaft of moonlight in his eyes. It seemed so bright and out-of-place, and he reached up for it with fingers that quivered, strained. It slipped through his hand like air, and he followed it upward with his gaze to the small, barred window high in the battered wall. Not often did light so penetrate his cell, for the penal colony was forever shrouded in darkness, situated opposite the world from its sun.

But tonight the light seemed to come from farther away than the three circling moons, even from beyond the black veil pierced by distant stars and unnamed galaxies.

A fierce shudder gripped him. His lips quaked, a word trying to fight its way onto his tongue. At first it was only a whisper, a groan, and then for the first time in a long while the sound of his own voice gurgled from his throat.

"Faroul!"

It's you! You're out there, waiting for someone with the power, waiting for me!

He lay there, letting the light bathe his face, strangely filling him with strength and will, until it became only a faint glow, then blackness.

A rat brushed his fingers. He listened to the rodent's high-pitched squeak, a noise like a door creaking on a rusty hinge. The sound intensified, echoing through the cell, and then he realized with senses deadened by the mysterious reaches of space that it was the cell block door opening.

He turned and light exploded into his eyes. There was no sensation of power, hope, this time, only pain. He groaned and squinted, his hand a screen before his eyes.

Chains rattled. "All right, put 'em on."

They clanged to the floor at his feet, and through parted fingers Alan found the silhouette of a large, brutish man with full beard. A meter-long club swayed in one brawny hand while the other grasped a handbeam.

He poked Alan in the ribs. "Hey, you hear me?" The gruff voice was as domineering as ever.

Alan pulled himself to his hip and reached for the chains. There were two sets, with heavy iron clamps. He sat up and buckled one set around his ankles, and then snapped the other in place on his wrists. They bit into his skin, already scarred to the bone.

"Gettin' kinda slow, ain't you? Pirate, hell. You couldn't spit on your own foot no more. Let's go. Move!"

Alan struggled to his feet, his knees quaking.

The large man cursed and spat a stream at Alan's sandals. It trickled down the side of his foot and stained his skin brown. The silhouette stuffed his handbeam in his belt, grasped Alan's shoulder like hooks gripping meat, and slung him toward the door. Ribs collided with wall, and Alan moaned and sank, the blood a rivulet from the corner of his mouth.

The man laughed and spat on the wall just above Alan's head. "Ain't got nothin' left no more, not even guts. A hell of a space pirate. Just a stinkin' swine."

The mind rays of the Rayolian Crystal may have sapped Alan's individuality, his very soul, but suddenly for the first time in a long while, something besides fear and loneliness gripped him. It was hatred, unbridled hatred at anyone, anything, that kept him from Faroul.

His forehead grew hot with blood and his eyes narrowed like a killer falcon's. The words would not come, his vocal cords unresponsive, but the thoughts were there.

I'll kill you for that. Somehow, some way, I swear I'll kill you for that!

"All right, get up. Move!"

The club slammed into Alan's shoulder. He groaned from deep inside, pain splitting his torso. For a moment, visions of Kasterfayette voicing the words of Faroul's power seized him, filling him with strength and hope, and then he dragged himself to his feet and staggered out the cell door.

Outside, his sandaled feet kicked up small clouds of sand as his dragging chains rasped along the ground. His lungs labored as they squeezed air from the mine dust. Eerie, wraith-like shadows moved with him, cast by the trio of jewel-like moons, and then he gained a place in line with men of common characteristics.

For a long while he had told himself he was not as they, that the mind probe and searing dust would not destroy him. But as the wind disheveled his stringy hair on this day, he realized that he was one of them in all respects. He was just as broken and haggard as those with stooped shoulders, shuffling gaits, cheekbones protruding like bone through drumhead.

About him rose the layered bluffs, carved away like wind-swept sand. But there was an orderliness about the erosion, for it had been accomplished not by wind and rain, but by sweat and muscle and lives. His own palms were scarred like craters, his fingers bent and deformed so that he could no longer straighten them. Pick-and-shovel handles had imbedded splinters, stark reminders even in moments of rest that he too would die here, that his wrinkled skin would perish away in face of mine dust that consumed like a malignancy.

Six months was the average here. Some could not last past a few weeks; others somehow held on to hope and reason long enough to live a year or two. Sometimes when his mind was not fully clouded, Alan wondered how long it had been for him, how much more torture he must endure before his heart and lungs stopped their labor. He remembered counting sleep periods the first month or two, and then the mind ray had cluttered his thoughts and rent his essence.

But things somehow seemed clearer today, though his breaths were just as heaving as always. With distress, he watched the hundreds of prisoners—insurrectionists, thieves, political dissenters, pirates— herded like cattle beneath the Rayolian Crystal and out into the mines.

Whip cracked against bare back. Curses rang out. Clubs slammed into rib cage. One white-haired prisoner dropped to the dust and lay very still on his side until a guard's boot met his shoulder, rolling him over to leave unseeing eyes staring skyward.

And what was all this for? To mine worthless Alos dust from one hill, and move it to another? There was no wealth for the United Star Systems to gain here; this was only endless punishment, one that eventually killed as surely as an energy bolt from a Banning semiautomatic.

The line carried him slowly, each prisoner passing in turn beneath the mind ray, emitted by a crystal suspended by electromagnetic forces four meters above the ground at an arch in the outer wall. At a distance, the crystal seemed so innocent: a fist-sized jewel of crimson and turquoise, its top-like whirl directing myriad-colored rays to the bodies of those who staggered beneath. When Alan was not subjected to its mind-bending properties for a sleep or two, he almost longed for it, longed to become lost in the explosion in his eyes, in the sensation that he no longer had to think, reason, be aware of pain.

But at the same time, the crystal was horrid, because whatever it was that made him an individual was being stolen from him.

No! He must fight it, fight it or die! He breathed in deeply the odor of sweaty bodies and noted how the wind chilled his arms even while bathing them in watery beads. He trudged nearer the crystal, nearer the decadent outer wall that stood against the outlying strip mines and desert. Beneath the flooding rays men knelt and cried, their vocal cords no longer able to emit intelligible words. The man in front of Alan lifted chained arms to the crystal and muttered incoherent incantations. It had become their god, their purpose in life. And for a long while it had been Alan's, until the memories of Kasterfayette's words had pushed it from his mind, told him of nobler things, greater gods.

Faroul! What had the old man's words been? He struggled to clear his mind, sweep away the cobwebs. *Power. Secret. Creation.* The words burst upon him like an exploding nova. *To the ones with the power goes the secret of creation!*

Abruptly he found himself beneath the crystal. He looked up, the rainbow of colors glinting in his eyes. *Damn you to hell! You can't take it! Not my mind, soul!*

The rays cascaded down, cleaving his skull. The force racked his cells, dissolving his thoughts into a swirling storm. No! His memories began to dim, his own self-identity disintegrating. Then a sudden vision of the light piercing his cell swept all else from his mind.

Faroul! His cells shrieked the word. His muscles tightened. His quaking fingers became a fist. *Faroul!*

A feeling of utter power, defiance, overwhelmed him. By strength of willpower, he drove back the rays, seeking to destroy them as they had destroyed him.

Faroul! The rays exploded in his eyes. He slung them across the sky, a multitude of colors dancing in the blackness like images in a shimmering pool. He felt his beaten and broken body straighten, as if filled with unearthly power. Then he stared at a mere fist-shaped jewel rendered motionless above, stared and laughed and knew that he had conquered.

Chapter Two

Alan stepped through the gate and followed the prisoners into the strip mines. He couldn't begin to understand what had happened to him. But for the first time in a long while he possessed acute self-awareness, the sense that he lived and contained a world of his own inside, one that never could be taken away again.

As if awakening from a deep sleep punctuated by nightmare, he found himself looking at the bluffs ahead and realized that this was to be the day. Intuition told him as much, reassuring him that all was in order, that things would happen just as they should.

Chained prisoners brushed past, their sweat mixing with his. Through dust that stung his eyes, he watched guards distribute picks and shovels to the subdued men with lifeless faces. Fully a thousand had now entered the mines to sling iron against rock, to build blister upon blister and bruise upon aching muscle. And guarding them? A mere handful of United Star Systems troopers with club, whip, and Banning.

That was all. Nothing else, neither walls nor armies nor any other terror separated them from the desert lowlands that became like a fog in the distance.

It seemed strange that he should never have realized before just how greatly prisoners outnumbered troops in this penal colony. As metal struck rock and whip cracked against flesh, he glanced back at the crystal. That jewel, and it alone, kept prisoners docile—had kept *him* docile—and would continue to do so until blessed death.

No! They would not do it to him! Never again! He would reach the desert where lay only dry ground and Alosian cacti. And something else.

Freedom! It became a silent cry of hope that evolved into a guttural deep in his throat.

A sharp pain pierced his upper ribs. He whirled to see club receding, and he glared into the close-set eyes of the bearded guard who had hustled him out of his cell. His own eyes narrowed, the blood pounding in his forehead.

Lines furrowed the guard's brow, as if he read in Alan's face something that the Rayolian Crystal should have robbed. The jailer hesitated, running a finger through a greasy beard tangled like cobwebs.

"You. What are you doin'?" The inflection of his voice hinted of deeper questions.

For long seconds the wind swept the guard's hair and tossed his purple-and-gold uniform. Then Kasterfayette's words came to Alan, growing in intensity until they roared like nuclear engines. His muscles tensed as power surged through him, a mere tingle that evolved into an explosion through every molecule.

Not now! he cried to himself. *Not here! Not when they can see!*

He lowered his head, forcing his eyes to become blank, and listlessly slunk deeper into strip mines.

The work period passed slowly, with only the moons' progression across the heavens to indicate the passage of time. Dehydration swelled Alan's tongue. Brittle rock struck his shins with every impact of his pick. Worn sandals rubbed heels like sandpaper as he shoved ore into gondolas. One by one, those about him began to collapse, to die and be dragged away to the pit at the desert's edge.

The largest of the three moons had just touched the guard tower on the western horizon when a frail prisoner with protruding rib cage dropped at Alan's feet. The unfortunate man began to foam at the mouth, and then vomited and convulsed.

Alan watched the spasms rack his frame like shock treatments. To die in the dust, a worthless pawn in an interstellar game of hate and revenge . . . That was the only peace the man would find, the only solace any of them would know.

Except him!

He waited until the eyes rolled up into their sockets and the body became still before lifting his gaze to the bearded guard, standing a few meters away with whip coiled snake-like. Their eyes met, and in question, Alan touched the dead man's shoulder with shovel point.

A second guard with features veiled by dark, streaming hair nudged the bearded man. "He's dead."

They approached. The bearded jailer spat a juicy stream to the puddle of vomit beside the body. "Flies are bad," he commented. He rubbed his nose into his shoulder. "Better get him to the pit."

The long-haired guard nodded to Alan. "No use us working. Not when that pig can do it."

"He don't have enough left to drag himself."

Nevertheless, the jailer with streaming hair looked at Alan and nodded to the corpse. "Pick him up."

Something clicked inside Alan's mind: a forgotten memory, momentary *déjà vu*, something he couldn't quite grasp.

"He said drag him!" The unshaven man's voice was gruff, and he came closer, beard twitching, fingers playing along the club.

Alan relaxed his grip on the shovel and let it clang to the ground. As his chains rattled, he knelt on shaky legs and slid his hands under the dead man's shoulders from behind. Vomit trickled down his wrist, and he could feel the still-warm skin against his own. One moment there had been two worlds, and the next, only his own. It was so easy to die here, and so difficult to live.

The four persons interwoven by fate—two guards, a dead prisoner and a dying one—made their way down the eroded hills, past creaking ore freighters and heavily laden gondolas that grated along tracks. In the foursome's wake, the heels of the dead man slashed a trail in the dirt.

After long minutes, the men reached the final strip mine, where the bearded guard grunted and motioned to a path cut by heels of other dead men. The trail carried Alan toward the desert flats, and as he weakened under his burden, he glanced at the cacti silhouetted in the distance. When he reached the first cluster, he found the cacti brooding over an open mass grave like spirits of the dead. From below, the stench of death rose up, searing his nasal passages.

He stopped at the precipice as dirt sloughed to the carnage ten meters below. Raw meat formed twisted mounds, leaving slashing gullies between. Fist-sized Alosian maggots swarmed over gnarled bones, bloated stomachs, tongues misshapen like pus-filled ulcers. On hunks of flesh perched several white vultures, ripping sinew with their long talons.

With Alan's new-found awareness, he cringed in realization that these were human bodies, temples of being and soul. It seemed so senseless an end, such a shattering of hopes and dreams. But like all those who toiled in these hills and fought the rats in the dungeons, this had long been his own horrid destiny.

The long-haired guard stopped beside him and peered over the edge, but the bearded jailer immediately crowded Alan.

"Throw him over," he snapped. "Watch how you're gonna end up, you swine."

Like hell!

A vision of Faroul surged through Alan, again promising strange power, and this time he didn't restrain it. In a millisecond the power raced through him, a multitude of exploding novas culminating in a primal scream.

The body became light, a club in his arms. He slammed it against the long-haired guard, dead sinew pounding living tissue. With a loud *oomph!,* the jailer stumbled at precipice's edge, his foot creating a landslide. For a moment time seemed to stand still and his eyes met Alan's, and then he plummeted into the shadows.

"Bastard!" cried the bearded man, reaching for his Banning.

Alan wrenched the firearm from the guard's fingers, but he could do nothing about the cudgel that crashed down. He dodged, catching a glancing blow in the shoulder that only made him more determined. With chain in hand, he leaped for the shaggy beard and bludgeoned the man in the temple, dazing him enough to wrap chain around neck from behind.

The guard struggled desperately to pry the crushing steel from his larynx. He drove his boot heel into Alan's shin, dropping him to dangle at chain's length. Then they both were down, the starry sky a maelstrom as they tumbled into the ravine.

They slammed into the bottom as the bones of the dead shattered beneath. The two men's skulls collided, the guard catching the worst of it. A maggot grazed Alan's face as he raised his head, trying to clear his senses. He found the bearded man lying very still, a cadaver's crushed rib cage cradling his head.

Freeing the chain from the thick neck, Alan found blood and bits of skin clinging to the links like flesh on meat hooks. As he came to his elbow, he started, struck by a strange sensation that something was amiss.

He whirled. Nearby lay the other guard, dazed but fumbling with his holster strap.

With a growl of revenge, Alan dived for his throat. The long-haired man cried out and threw up an arm to fend him off. Alan's chains slammed through his defense and found the guard's cheekbone, and then the two rolled into a shallow canyon of flesh. Sinew wrestled sinew as maggots gathered, but Alan gained the upper hand and tightened his fingers around the guard's throat.

The man's eyes bulged as he broke Alan's hold long enough to utter a single word. Alan heard, but somehow the cry failed to register, even though it pricked something deep inside him. Determined, he regained his throat hold, and yet at the same time he dwelled on what he had heard.

It came upon him like a spasm, setting him trembling as he relaxed his grip, his mind a bewildering blend of thought, emotion, memory.

"Alan!"

It was his own name being voiced, a word he had not heard in eons, one he had almost forgotten.

"For God's sake, Alan!"

The guttural crawled up from the man's nearly crushed throat and Alan drew back, squinting in confusion. He leaned against a hollow-eyed skull and stared as the jailer rolled away, coughing horribly and rubbing his throat. Alan reached for his shoulder, a thousand questions in the touch, and the man came to his elbow and faced him.

Through the moonlight, Alan saw him clearly for the first time: the slightly off-center nose, eyebrows like miniature forests, cheekbones raised as if wanting to burst through flesh, the chin with a trench-like crease.

Suddenly Alan was not a shell of a man half-buried in maggot-ridden corpses on a desolate penal colony. He was an eternity away in time and space. Captain. A bloodthirsty group of cutthroats and insurrectionists under his command. Starship controls at his fingers. And at his side, with eyes filled with awe and fear, a trembling boy, the sole survivor of a cruel massacre of a dozen families whose transport errantly had crossed into a United Star Systems military zone.

"L-Lin-Lindsay!"

The young man reached for his bony arm. "I . . . I came for you, Captain." His lips quaked, his hoarse voice filled with emotion. He smiled. "I always knew they couldn't break you. Anybody else, but not you."

"I . . ." Alan's words would not come, the vocal cords not responding. "How . . ."

Lindsay shrugged. "I'm here. That's all that matters."

The young man surveyed the eddies of dust on the rim above, and then secured a key from his belt and unlocked Alan's chains. As the links dropped, a sense of impending freedom lifted Alan's spirits to unimaginable heights.

Lindsay helped him to his feet and nodded to the far rim. "I've got a flyer, out in the desert. Hurry!"

Alan staggered, and Lindsay's arm became a supporting brace as they turned to the sloping bluff a dozen meters away. As they waded through the carnage, a thousand thoughts swam crazily through Alan's mind, forcing him to test the reality of the moment. Then something stirred at his feet, and he looked down and found the first guard's shoulders shining in the moonlight. The beard began to twitch, the eyes to blink.

The brush of Lindsay's holstered Banning against his leg brought Alan's gaze to the weapon. He seized it, and somehow it seemed as if he never had been without one. Shaking free of his companion, he whirled and leveled the Banning on the bearded man's cruel features.

"What the—" Lindsay turned, obviously not understanding.

Alan's finger tightened on the pressure release. *Die, you bastard.*

An ineffably bright mass of blue light exploded before him, leaving electromagnetic static crackling in the wind. The smell of burned flesh joined the odor of rotting meat, and when the stars stopped dancing inside Alan's head, only the bearded man's charred body lay in his sights.

Lindsay tore the weapon from his grasp. "Let's go!" he cried. "The guards, they'll all be after us!"

As Lindsay dragged him away, Alan glanced back at the dead guard and smiled in grim satisfaction.

Chapter Three

Sweeping across barren desert, the wind snaked sand about Alan's ankles and rippled his tattered clothes. His mouth was as dry as the baked ground, and with each step his legs grew weaker.

He clutched Lindsay's arm, digging his nails into skin. He coughed, staggered, and sank to the young man's boots. He lay there, the starry expanse spinning overhead.

Lindsay was tugging at him, his lips forming words that seemed to come from a great distance. But Alan couldn't respond, for he was lost in shadowy forms that danced inside his eyelids.

"Fight!" Lindsay was saying. "We've got it made! Just fight this one last time!"

The inner blackness overwhelmed Alan. His thoughts meshed with the innumerable colors of the Rayolian Crystal, exploding through the universe, and he seemed to become something more in dream and idea than he ever had been before. Later, he would remember only vague snippets of reality: his heels plowing through dust, his arms dangling limply inside another's, Lindsay's boots clicking against metal, hands bolting a pressure door, untold G forces pushing against his body.

It was this last sensation that pricked his subconscious so intensely: the crush of larynx against throat, the shriek of every cell. He had been here before, but he was helpless to escape the surrealism.

As consciousness finally dawned, light flooded his eyes and he sensed the vibration of engines. He lay with his cheek against forearm, and something restrained him as he tried to roll to his side. Reaching down, he felt bands along his chest and calves.

A computer console with lights racing along circuits loomed before him, and he lifted his head and scanned his surroundings. Reclined on an anti-gravity couch nearby, a slender man with wavy hair and the uniform of a United Star Systems guard studied start charts, while the black reaches of space, dotted with miniscule stars, swept toward them through the broad forward porthole.

Alan lowered his head and closed his eyes. He had experienced such hallucinations before; the cold, dark cell ruled his mind during times of rest as surely as the Rayolian Crystal did in the mines.

But now when he opened his eyes again, the impressions only intensified: starship controls with multi-colored buttons and computer screens flashing red, the hum of nuclear engines, the odor of the vinyl couch beneath his head, the taste of artificially manufactured oxygen and nitrogen in the air.

And opposite him, a man rustling star maps.

It all came back in an instant, bringing with it another sensation: the ecstasy of freedom.

"Hope you don't have us lost, Lin." His voice was weak, hoarse, unfamiliar even to his own ears.

Lindsay whirled. "Alan!" He sat up and twisted his legs to the floor. "I knew you'd snap out of it. I've shot enough medication in you the past sixty hours to fill a freighter."

Alan ran his hand along the restraints. "Get these things off. I've had enough chains for a while."

Lindsay stood and unbuckled the straps. "Sorry. You've been tossing around so much I was afraid you'd get hurt."

When the young man helped him sit up, Alan's vision swam. He shook his head and dangled his legs to the floor. "How long? Two years? Three?"

Lindsay obtained a towel from a compartment and dabbed Alan's sweaty forehead. "My God, Alan, did it rob you of that much? It's been nine years."

Nine years! The words reverberated through Alan's mind, pierced every cell.

"No," he said quietly. "Two or three, but no more."

Lindsay pointed to the chronological readout in the console. "Take a look for yourself. I guess you must've lost all track in that hellhole."

Alan studied the figures for so long that they burned indelibly into his mind. "I . . . I didn't think it was possible," he said in disbelief. "Not with what I . . . not where I was."

"Neither did anybody else," said Lindsay.

Alan stood on rubbery legs. Lindsay caught him by the upper arm, and the older man could only shake his head. "Looks like it took more than just time from me," he whispered, studying his whip-scarred arms.

He surveyed Lindsay, the blue eyes hardened by the passage of years, the straightening of the jaw and chin that comes only with maturity. He smiled. "Last time I saw you, you were just a wild-eyed kid with a head full of ideas."

Lindsay shrugged. "You may think worse than that now." He nodded to the star charts on the couch, and then turned to the myriad suns and clusters through the glass nose of the ship. "It's out there, Alan. It's out there somewhere, and Poteet's going after it."

Alan drew back. "Poteet!" he exclaimed with contempt and hatred. "I swallowed mine dust for so long that I forgot a lot of things, but not him, not what he did."

He clenched his fist and stared into the blackness of space. For a moment, his mind drifted to a time long before he first had felt the Rayolian Crystal. As vividly as on that long ago day, he again saw Poteet sitting across a table from him, a flagon of intoxicating lemstel in his hands and saliva drooling down his tangled black beard.

Poteet was laughing, leaned back with his mouth open, revealing teeth like broken fence slats. Alan flinched at the bite of manacles in his wrists, cursed as a crush of U.S.S. guards dragged him across the floor. Then a brawny arm raised a club and Poteet's laughter went with him into oblivion.

Alan shook himself back to the present, but now a chill gnawed at his marrow. "No," he said finally. "He won't make it. Not to—"

"Talk's out in the black market all through the colonies that he's figured out the way, planning to go after it."

Alan glanced at the star charts and shook his head. "He'll never make it, not to Faroul. Nobody can. Nobody knows the way, except . . ."

He felt a sharp pain just above his brow. He sank to the couch and buried his face in his palms. His fingers, rough and bent, somehow seemed to soothe, as though by hiding within them, he could find peace, escape for an instant Kasterfayette's haunting words.

Lindsay's hand was soft on his shoulder. "You know the way, don't you? Of all the people in the colonies, in the universe, you're the only one that does."

Alan opened his eyes to his quivering hands. "I . . . I don't even know who I am anymore," he said quietly.

"That night when Poteet handed us over, I watched them drag you away and knew this wasn't the end of it. They put me away in a standard penitentiary on Ares IV. I got off light, being so young. When they let me out a few months ago, I hired on with a freighter, and every time we made port I'd go down into the black market sector and try to find out about Poteet, you."

Alan looked up, finding Lindsay's countenance growing even more serious.

"Alan, he's going to do it. I know he is."

"He couldn't be. That day, when Kasterfayette told me about Faroul, Poteet was in the quarters but I made him leave, leave to let the old man whisper."

"Are you sure Poteet didn't turn on the intercom on the way out?"

Alan stared into his eyes, remembering, and could not answer.

"You say he can't make it," said Lindsay, "that he doesn't know the way. Are you sure enough to risk letting him get that kind of power?"

Alan breathed sharply. "Everybody thinks they know so much. What power? Poteet doesn't know, and neither does the United Star Systems or all the scientists in the colonies."

He stood and stared at the computer readouts, and then turned to survey Lindsay's U.S.S. uniform, the gold strips against purple. "A good fit," he noted. "Looks like you had things fixed pretty good. How'd you do it?"

"A few bribes here and there. Once I found out you were still alive, it wasn't hard to put credits in the right hands and get on as a guard. Money drives a hard bargain."

"Almost as hard a one as power," observed Alan. For long moments, there was only the whine of the computer. "So you came for me. You came so I could stop Poteet."

"So *we* could. He sent me away to die too, you know. I thought you'd do anything, go to any lengths, to break his neck."

Alan's chest expanded. "I guess I would." He turned, studying the craft's interior. "Where'd you get it?"

"Black market."

"Steal it?"

Lindsay shook his head. "Made a deal. There's a battleship and crew to go along with it."

Alan frowned, and he took in every detail of the young man's face. "I think you'd better explain."

"Okay," said Lindsay, nodding. "Poteet sold us out to the United Star Systems and got us locked up. That left him to roam the colonies with a full pardon and enough credits to buy a solar system. But he wasn't satisfied. He wanted more. He started preying on government freighters again, then word was out he knew the way to Faroul, that he'd do anything to get there.

"I got released, found out all this, and it made me want to spill his guts even more for what he did to us. So I made a deal with pirates in the black market, that if they'd supply the crafts and crew, I'd spring you and we'd go after Poteet."

"What did you promise them?"

"Faroul."

Alan made a fist. "That's too much." He turned to the couch. His vision had begun to fade, and another sharp pain struck his temple. He lay down and closed his eyes, and for a moment he was lost again in the dungeons, the feel of rats scurrying across his legs.

When he looked up, Lindsay hovered over him as if studying his wrinkled face, the hair streaked with white. "Our contact, he's in Thalia," said Lindsay. "And out there across the galaxy, Poteet may be waiting for us."

"There's something else out there too, Lin. It's been waiting for a long time, forever." Alan sat up, wild with memories of the light in his cell. "*Faroul. It wants something, Lindsay. It wants me!*"

Lindsay folded his arms across his chest as if to fight it away an inexplicable coldness. He seemed anxious to ask more, about Kasterfayette, about the secret of creation. But Alan knew that his mysterious words must have dissuaded him. What was out there that could so possess a person who had never even seen it?

Alan was afraid that one day the answers would come.

Chapter Four

The Rogues' Tavern was not unlike any other dingy palace of delights in the black market sector of Thalia, largest city on the U.S.S. colony Zara II. It reeked with the same foul lemstel brew and identical leche weed smoke that spiraled upward from black-stemmed pipes to settle on beard and face, rumpled clothes and bare skin.

Here, the outcasts and scum of the colonies gathered to barter, scheme, and betray. And here too, they tried to escape, through mind-warping drugs or the illicit pleasures found in rooms of delight beyond the golden curtains that shimmered like the veils of half-naked girls who danced to Thalian lyres.

It was late. The shapely woman of thirty, with silky, chestnut hair dangling halfway down her back, sat on the edge of a velvety mattress supported a meter above the floor by jets of air. From beyond the closed door came the sounds of revelry against a background of exotic music. The lyres seemed to have an intoxicating effect on her tonight, and she closed her eyes and swayed gently to the beat.

It was warm, and she could feel rivulets trickling down her forehead. And yet it was as if a chill enveloped her, raising bumps on her arms and spine, and when she opened her eyes she saw her fingers trembling through a cloud of wavy hair.

She smoothed out the sheer, white tunic that left a V of skin along each thigh. Her palms grew moist, and she ran her fingers nervously along the gold trim. And quietly, as though it were the trickle of a stream submerged in the roar of starship engines, her mother's voice echoed in her memory.

"Away! Go away from me, from all of us!"

She saw herself, wrenched by grief, fall at her mother's feet and reach up with pale hands, imploring. *"Mother!"* she cried, her voice racked by fear. *"Help me! Oh, Mother, you've got to help me!"*

But the rocks continued to pummel, searing her with pain, and her cries were drowned by the curses and chants of her people, her family, her mother.

"Die, witch!" they screamed as stones slammed into her back, shoulders, legs. *"Die!"*

A rock glanced off her skull and she sank to the dust, hearing the voices grow less distinct. Still, the stones continued to jerk her body like electrical shocks. She looked up with bloodied eyes and found one particular silhouette against the blinding sun, and the last thing she remembered was the splatter of her mother's spittle in her face.

She looked toward the door, her gaze fixing on the shiny metallic knob. Her mind became a confusing blend of reality and dream, what was and what might be. It was as if something inside her clicked, granting her momentary awareness of things beyond, allowing her to see down a long roadway and discern which paths led to certain destinations, certain events.

Now, as often before, she saw the knob turn an instant before it did, heard too soon the door screech open, saw the dirty, scowling man with gray-streaked mustache walk through before it happened.

The knob turned. The door opened with a creak like new leather pulled taut. And framed in the doorway was the very man she had anticipated. He stormed in, the pyramidal ceiling light glinting in his greasy hair as the door slammed behind him.

Paling, she drew back.

"What the hell you doin', you—!" he demanded with a choice epithet.

She jumped up. "Get away from me!"

Another epithet exploded from the man's thin lips and he started toward her with evil intent. She whirled, looking for a place to go. The couch behind her, with air jets whistling. A closet at her left. A cracked window yielding the stench of the alley.

When she spun again, the man was in her face, his foul breath suffocating as he seized the breast of her tunic.

"A black market kingpin and you're too good for him?" he charged. "I oughta—"

"I don't care *who* he was," she said defiantly. "He comes in, tries to knock me around. I'm not here for stuff like that."

The man flushed with rage. "You're here 'cause I found you in the desert, bleedin', half-dead! You're here 'cause I give you a roof over your head, two meals a day, four credits a trick! You're here so all the scum of the colonies can use you! Just what *else* you think you're good for?"

"I . . . I don't have to get knocked around like that."

He backhanded her in the mouth. "The hell you don't!"

She dropped to the floor, her lip stinging. Looking up, she found him silhouetted against the overhead light in much the same way her mother had been against the sun.

"You're gonna do the same thing you been doin' all these years," he said. "Sleep till noon, go flaunt yourself, find you some scum. You're gonna do whatever they want, take their money, and give it to me.

"You owe me a lot, you whore, and you're payin' up. Startin' with the black marketer again."

He burst out of the room, leaving a grim quietness.

The woman sobbed, now that he could no longer derive sadistic pleasure from it, and found blood on her lip. As she lay quaking in anger and fear, the pyramidal light captured her attention. At first a mist blurred her eyes, but as she stared, the light began to assume shape.

It was a skull-sized vessel of dense Zaran gas, pulsating blue, then white, with energy. She concentrated on it, taking in every detail: the finely hewn star-age glass, the meter-long chain that supported it from the ceiling, its slight sway in a wind that whistled through the cracked window.

Suddenly it seemed she could see beyond the brightness and discern images, places, persons: a road here, a path elsewhere. She saw a man with atrophied muscles, mine dust on his skin, and powerful forces in his mind that spoke of freedom, power, destiny. The images were clouded by time and decisions yet unmade, but they were there, and so was she. They were together, hand in hand, and they stood before a wall of fire.

She started, her skin turning clammy. She shook her head and tried to clear her vision, but the images she had seen so often before were still strong, piercing her very soul. Abruptly, a single word encompassed her every thought, as if there were nothing else in the universe.

Faroul!

She was scared, because now she saw the start of the path toward it, and she knew what she had to do.

She gained her feet and crossed the room quickly, stopping at the clothes drawers built into the wall. She ran her hand down the brass knobs, halting on the third. Pulling it open, she rummaged inside with unsteady fingers as her heart pounded like blows from a fist.

Where was it? It had to be here!

She found only undergarments, stockings, jewelry before the click of boot heels outside sliced through her. Whirling, she saw the inside latch give.

She couldn't find it!

The door screeched open. At the last instant, her fingers found a sharp blade with an ornately carved handle. Pulling it free, she spun to conceal it behind her in a moist palm.

A heavy-set man with missing teeth picked his nose and grinned as a dog might have done in eyeing a hunk of meat. "Seems we've been through this before, you cheap little whore."

Almost gently, he closed the door and started toward her. She took in every detail in his face: the two-day growth of beard, the bushy eyebrows, the ugly black mole on his jaw. But his dark, close-set eyes struck her most, for they were those of a predator that had cornered its prey. She drew back, dagger meeting wall.

"You know," he began quietly, loosening his belt and continuing his approach, "I've been with a lot of whores, a lot that cried and whined, but you're the first with any guts."

He pulled his belt free and grasped it by the buckle so that the leather dangled like an uncoiled serpent. He spat between his teeth, leaving a brown splotch on the floor between them. "Know somethin'? It's the ones like you that *really* need a man to knock hell out of 'em."

The woman turned as cold as a derelict ship in orbit, but as she flexed anxious fingers on the dagger, she forced a seductive smile and motioned with her head. "Come here," she said, calling upon all the years of coyness that had been so important to her trade. "We'll do something special, just for you."

"You damned right we will."

He was before her now, and she could smell the lemstel on his breath and the leche smoke on his clothes. He snaked the belt about her thighs, the calm before a storm.

Suddenly he seized her hair, forcing her head back so that her face was vulnerable. She cried out, and then the buckle's sharp edge was at her cheek.

He snickered cruelly. "I'm gonna cut you up so bad *nobody'll* want you."

She flinched and tried to struggle free. He jerked her head savagely. His obscenities were in her ears. The dagger grew taut in her hand. As if she were outside the world looking in, she saw the blade flash free, glinting in the light, saw it drive deep into the chest of the man and withdraw dripping red with blood.

***

The ship's chronometer registered minutes, hours, days, but there was no rising and setting of a sun to mark the passage of time. There were only its effects—the growth of a beard on Alan's face, hunger pangs, tiredness—as well as a progression of events. They ate, slept, checked instruments, made navigational corrections, and talked.

They were aboard a small military fighter, swift and efficient for strikes against rebel bases and carrier starships, but also cramped. There was little room for exercise, only rest, and Alan slowly regained minimal strength. But it was a struggle. The muscles were deadened, the flesh stretched over rib cage like tanned leather. His gait was slow and labored, and the weakness in his knees remained. But his mind was becoming less cluttered with irrational thoughts, and now he could sit at the controls, stare into the clouds of the Milky Way, and tell himself that after all these years he was alive again and had an identity of his own.

It was three days by chronometer when the star system Zara loomed close, its sun a fiery orb adrift in a sea of ebony. Alan sat at the console instruments, reacquainting himself with their use, and glanced at the seven orbiting planets: crimson, green, and blue jewels studding a solar crown. They were still many hours away, even at starship speed, and he felt a sudden sense of awe. It was as if he saw himself from afar, a microscopic speck in cosmic vastness, a speck as insignificant to the whole as a grain of sand to an ocean.

Planets. Star systems. Galaxies. Galactic clusters. Infinity.

And he, a dying shell, watching an entire universe die with him.

He looked at Lindsay, who sat running computer checks. "You know, Lin, sitting here just now, I don't guess I ever really looked at all of that and realized just how much it and I have in common." He nodded to the starry expanse.

Something in his voice obviously piqued Lindsay's interest, for the younger man scooted back and surveyed him. "What do you mean?"

Alan's vision grew indistinct, the sun becoming a fuzzy ball and the distant stars shimmering crosses. "We both used to be something we're not anymore, something we can't ever be again."

"Why don't you get some rest, Alan."

Alan shook his head. "What's the current ratio of dead stars—white dwarfs—to live ones in our galaxy? Ten to one? Twelve?"

Lindsay shrugged. "Something like that."

Alan nodded. "It's getting to be a graveyard out there, Lin. Stars are born, they grow old, and die, just like us." He turned and his expression was solemn as he stared at the younger man. "Think about it. All those immense giants out there, stars that dwarf us like we don't even exist, and they're not any better off than we are. We die, and they die too. And there's nothing in the universe that can ever change it. It's like death is the great equalizer. It brings us up to their level, and them down to ours."

Lindsay nodded to the couch. "Go ahead and lay down. We'll be in orbit before you know it."

The younger man's voice seemed distant, faint. As Alan looked across the trackless reaches of the galaxy, a sudden memory of a strong, quiet voice pricked him. *"The heavens will wax old like a garment."*

The voice was his father's, the words from ancient Hebrew writings, and Alan shuddered.

"Something I've wanted to ask you." Lindsay's words brought him aware. "Back there, the mass grave. We'd've gotten away clean. Nobody would've known. Why'd you have to kill him?"

Alan's chest rose and beads of sweat broke out along the back of his hands. He looked ahead at the approaching star system and clenched his fingers. "Because he did me wrong."

The series of planets began to fade, the hum of the computer seemed to cease, and he remembered.

He was nine years old, and tears rolled down his cheeks. A heavy lump had lodged in his throat, and there was a pain deep inside his temples.

In his hands was a small Rhythian falcon, its black feathers silky smooth, its talons hard and curved like its long beak. But there was something more, something savage: its head was crushed, the blood drying on the down in its neck.

He stood in the doorway of the modest rock dwelling with steps descending a meter into the living quarters, where a clean-featured young man with dark hair and blue eyes sat reading a Bible before a fireplace.

The boy looked down at the dead bird and sobbed. The air suddenly felt very cold, like the winter wind that swept snowflakes across the yard.

The man turned, saw, and came to his feet. "Alan? What's wrong?"

The boy ran his fingers along the smooth feathers, felt a tremor pass through his hands. "They killed him, Father. Killed him!"

Hanging his head, he closed his eyes as they continued to well. Within moments, he felt his father's hand soft on his shoulder, felt the warmth and comfort that only he could bring.

The young man knelt and ran his fingers along Alan's hand and on to the bloodied feathers. "Who, Alan? Who killed Alexiv?"

The boy's eyes were open, filled with hatred. He nodded to the door. "On the street, the boys. They beat him with a stick, killed him."

His father gathered him in his arms. "Oh, Alan, I'm sorry. I'm so sorry!" he said with choked voice. "I know how you loved him, cherished him."

The boy buried his face into his father's shoulder and clenched his teeth. "I grabbed the stick and chased them," he said angrily. "I hit every one till they fell down crying, begging me to stop!"

His father withdrew far enough to look into Alan's face, which must have shown rage and bitterness. "But Alan, you know we shouldn't do something like that when someone wrongs us. We're supposed to forgive, pray for them. The Bible says we should help them so they won't go to hell."

The boy looked down at the lifeless bird and at the dried blood in his palm. He made a fist and felt his heart pound viciously. "I should've killed them," he rasped, "killed them and made *sure* they went to hell!"

And he swore that next time he would.

Chapter Five

Rain fell in torrents, leaving Alan's hair straightened and dripping as his footsteps echoed through the east Thalian slums. He felt a sense of unease, as though something evil lurked nearby, but there was only Lindsay beside him, Lindsay and the skid row lemstel addicts crowding the shadows.

As Alan drew his collar together against a cold wind and sloshed through muddy puddles, he looked at the younger man. "This place, this contact. Who is he?"

"His name's Juarez." Rain struck the brick roadway in regular rhythm. "He's just a petty little pirate wanting more than he can get any other way."

Alan wiped the beads from his face. "Sounds like the kind that'd do anything to get it."

Lindsay shrugged. "He's the one I got the fighter from and the money to bribe my way into Alos. I think he's on the up and up."

Alan shook his head. "The mention of Faroul puts lots of ideas in people's heads, turns good men into petty thieves and petty thieves into demons."

"You make it sound like we're fixing to get our throats slit."

Alan stopped and looked at him gravely. "If you promised them Faroul, that's just what will happen when they find out they can't have it."

Lindsay had halted with him. "I don't understand about Faroul, about you. You were the last person to talk to Kasterfayette, you and Poteet. What was it he told you?"

Alan looked ahead through the misty darkness. "Not everybody can have Faroul," he said quietly.

For long seconds, there was only the pummeling of the rain as it washed debris down gutters. "Just who *can* have it, Alan? Can you? Can we?"

Alan only trudged onward through the downpour.

***

Alan could smell the leche weed and lemstel long before they reached the tattered doorway of the Rogues' Tavern, where a prostitute eyed him seductively as she leaned against the threshold. It had been a long time since he had seen a woman, smelled her perfume, felt her warmth within his arms, but it had been too long. The dungeons had robbed him of so many things; all that remained were memories, dreams.

Breathing deeply the odor of intoxicants that stung his throat, he followed Lindsay down the steps to find boisterous activity within. A scantily clad Thalian girl danced to lyre and flute. Men whooped and argued. Lemstel flowed freely, from barrel to flagon to lips and beard. The shadows swirled with leche weed smoke. Beyond the tables and bar lay wispy gold curtains, through which prostitutes led men with lusting eyes, roaming hands.

Next to a pillar in a murky corner, Lindsay found a table strewn with empty flagons and stained with lemstel. As Alan followed, he noted the crowding faces: the gaunt and the broad, the bearded and the smooth, the wide eyes and the hollow ones. Every one of them seemed lost in mind-warping drugs, trying to escape the very reality Alan had sought to hold on to the last nine years.

He sat down opposite Lindsay and looked at the reflection of the purple wall-candles in the spilled lemstel. He tendered a hand to the brownish liquid, and then withdrew it and glanced at the tavern's patrons and prostitutes.

"I wish they knew," he muttered. He looked at Lindsay. "I wish you knew."

Lindsay motioned for a sunken-eyed waiter with a tray of lemstel. "Knew what?"

Alan remembered the rats on his legs, his own waste beneath his thighs, the dreams and visions spawned by the Rayolian Crystal. "That of all things in the universe, reality is the most important."

The waiter stopped before the table and surveyed them with tired eyes.

"Two lemstels," said Lindsay.

The man set down a pair of flagons as the brew sloshed over the edges. Lindsay extended credits and a tiny black stone. "Give it to the Korean at the bar."

The waiter eyed him quizzically, and then took the jewel and ambled toward the bar.

Lindsay turned the flagon to his lips and drank anxiously, letting the liquid run down the corners of his mouth. Alan stared at his own flagon, watching the lemstel shimmer like an eddying river. Strangely, he seemed to see his reflection: a pirate captain taking a scared boy under his wing and trying to inject some truth, some reality, in a cruel and heartless world.

"Just think, Alan!" the young man exclaimed. "If we get this set up, we've got it. We've got Poteet and a chance for Faroul. God, it puts chill bumps down my back."

Now, Alan looked only at Lindsay. "You've changed."

"What's that mean?"

"Back then, when you were a boy, you were so idealistic, sincere. Now you seem cynical, wanting too much, wanting to lose yourself in escape, power."

Lindsay lowered his flagon. "Sounds like you're talking about yourself," he said with a note of resentment. Already, the fast-acting intoxicant was taking effect. "You were the one that always hated the empire, swore you'd fight them till you died."

Alan nodded to the flagon. "The lemstel, why did you start?"

Lindsay drank long and hard, obviously savoring the taste. "Why not? It's a way to live, a way to make meaning out of crap."

"No," said Alan, "not meaning. There's only meaning when you forget about yourself, do something for somebody else."

Lindsay exhaled strongly. "I came for you, didn't I?"

Still, Alan stared. "For me, or for Faroul?"

Lindsay's hand flinched on the flagon. "Who are you to question my motives? A lot of good *you* did for others when you blew up all those U.S.S. freighters, killed all those men. Just who do you think you were doing all that for?"

Alan lowered his gaze to the lemstel stains and thought about his father, remembered and felt the blood course through his arteries like fuel in a rocket.

"Well, see you made it after all."

A gravelly voice sounded at Alan's shoulder. He turned to see a large man with full red beard and swarthy skin standing at his side, a Banning dangling from his hip and club-like arms folded across a barrel chest.

"Juarez!" exclaimed Lindsay.

The man took a long drag from a leche weed pipe, and then exhaled through his nose to send smoke curling upward. "Who's this skinny white trash with you?"

Alan's blood ran hot, and he scooted back his chair with a screech and started to rise.

"Alan!" Lindsay was on his feet, reaching for his arm. "Forget it. He didn't mean nothing by it."

Alan glared at the stranger. "Didn't he?"

Juarez laughed quietly. "You must be him. Nobody else as skinny and beaten would have that kind of nerve."

Lindsay pulled out a chair, preempting further words. "Sit down. We've got a lot to talk about." He eased down and cast imploring eyes on Alan.

Juarez sat, placed greasy elbows on the table, and took another drag on the pipe. "Faroul, huh?" he said skeptically. He nodded toward Alan. "Just what makes you think *he* can get us there, this feeble old man?"

"One with more guts than you'll *ever* have," snapped Alan.

Juarez eyed him. "So you think you know the way. You think we can stop Poteet, get there first."

For an extended moment, there was only the low beat of a drum as a girl stripped to the crowd's vulgar cries. "I made nine years on Alos."

Juarez turned to Lindsay. "Okay, but get one thing straight." His jabbed his finger into the young man's chest. "You double-cross me, you so much as think about it, and I'll spill your guts. Both of yours. Now you promised us Faroul. Live up to your end of the bargain and we'll live up to ours."

He glanced at Alan, and then turned fiery eyes back to Lindsay. "I hate your guts already. Nothing I'd like better than pull 'em out with my bare hands."

Alan remembered the dungeon guard and smiled defiantly. "You know something, Juarez? I've always enjoyed killed arrogant pigs like you."

There was more to be said, much more from either side, but Lindsay was suddenly between the two. "Hey! We've got Faroul waiting out there for us, Faroul and all that it promises. Why don't we just work together? This is the only chance we'll ever get."

Juarez obviously was not fully persuaded. "If anything's not on the up and up, I'll—"

"Where's the crew? The ship?" interjected Lindsay.

Juarez's eyes flashed for long seconds, and then he took another puff on the pipe and his features relaxed a little. "The desert outside the city. Eight kilometers. Twelve degrees west of north, the rock monolith that juts up."

"Heard any more about Poteet?" pressed Lindsay.

"They say he's been working the Myolian system, giving the freighters all they can handle. He's probably on his way to Faroul right now. With us still sittin' here."

"When will we meet?"

"Daybreak." He stood to leave, and the smoke rose with him. Turning, he slung a finger in Alan's face. "Somethin' else. I'm leader of this bunch. One word from me and my men will blast your—"

Alan slapped the hand away. "Don't give me that," he snapped. "I know what your men are: a bunch of petty pirates who'd slit their grandmother's throat or anybody else's for a profit. And that includes yours."

Juarez went crimson as his fingers played along his Banning strap.

"We'll be there," Lindsay blurted. "You can count on us."

Juarez's beard twitched for long seconds, but finally he wheeled and walked away.

Lindsay watched until he disappeared among the patrons, and then he whirled to Alan. "What are you trying to do? You know what almost happened?"

"Yeah," said Alan matter-of-factly. "I almost killed him."

Lindsay sighed. "You think you're that tough, don't you? You think you can spend nine years locked up in a cell block breathing mine dust and still do anything you used to. You always were that way, thinking nobody could stop you."

"I'm alive, aren't I?" returned Alan. "Where do you think *you'd* be if it wasn't for me being so tough? When I rescued you off that derelict transport, you were weak, starving, almost suffocated. Your whole family was dead just because of a navigational error. If I hadn't been so tough against the U.S.S. starship that blew your parents to pieces, you wouldn't be here today. So cut the crap."

Lindsay slammed his flagon against the table and stood. "You worry about what you want to. I've got my own worries." He looked across the tavern and sighted a blonde prostitute. "I see what I want right now."

He stormed away and left Alan alone with the glistening lemstel and troubling thoughts. In one way, he regretted what he had said. It had been the truth, all right, but truth sometimes hurt all parties involved. Wasn't Lindsay his only friend in all the colonies and star systems of the United Star Systems? Hadn't Lindsay risked his very life to save him from a hellhole?

As he stared into the lemstel, it seemed as if he no longer were surrounded by people, no longer heard the grate of chair against floor or the cries of the surly crowd as the dancing girl swayed to alien music. There were only he and the dying old man Kasterfayette, reaching for his arm, the long fingernails biting into his flesh and the sunken eyes widening with visions no other had ever beheld.

Alan shuddered, awed by the memory. "Creation," he whispered, and memories of the intense light flooding his cell filled his mind.

He started, his mind reeling with words that weren't his, words that called forth ancient scrolls, esoteric legends.

Power! Creation! Faroul!

He spun, sensing thoughts that were foreign, beyond the limits of what a man should know. A few meters away, framed in crispations of smoke between stone pillars, a woman stood staring at him. A chill crept down his spine, and then a strange, soothing warmth replaced it.

She was just a prostitute, he knew, one with smooth cheeks, flowing chestnut hair, white tunic that accentuated her figure. But there was something about her eyes that captivated him, each speck of green sparkling with knowledge, depth, power.

She came nearer, the candlelight playing along her glossed lips, and each graceful step revealed supple thighs through slits on either side of her tunic. Lord, she was beautiful, he thought. Silky legs. Narrow hips. Full breasts straining at their bonds. Eyelashes highlighted with mascara, cheeks tinged ever so lightly with rouge.

She stopped before him, and he could taste her tantalizing Thalian perfume. She glanced at the front entrance, beyond the stirring lemstel addicts, and stared into his eyes.

"Danger," she whispered. "There's danger here."

He looked about the tavern, studying it through the leche smoke, and then fixed his gaze on her. "What do you mean?"

She put her hand on his shoulder, delicate white fingers against blue flight uniform. "Come on," she said, nodding toward the sheer curtains. "You've got to hurry."

Alan took in her svelte body and shook his head. "I don't have any money."

She glanced apprehensively at the entrance and tugged on his arm. "Hurry!" she repeated quietly.

Again, Alan surveyed the tavern and found nothing amiss. Who was this woman? What could she want with him, other than his credits? He remembered how Poteet had trapped and betrayed him. How was he to know but that she planned to lure him into a similar snare?

She bent close, until her hair touched his cheek and the fragrance of her perfume intoxicated him. "Faroul," she whispered.

His eyes widened. A dozen questions came to his tongue, and then died on his lips.

He stood and followed her through the swirling smoke.

Chapter Six

Alan watched the swaying of her hips, noting how the sheer tunic outlined her charms. They brushed past brawny-armed traders and ebony-skinned Thalians, dodged strewn chairs and pools of lemstel, skirted the bar where glassy-eyed men fingered flagons and stared dully at flickering candles above wooden kegs.

A swarthy arm reached out from a swinging half-door at bar's end and clutched the woman. "Your last trick. Where the hell's my credits?" The scowling bartender with gray-streaked mustache grasped her tunic, his stumpy fingers groping her cleavage.

Alan had never seen the woman until mere seconds before, yet he suddenly wanted no other man in the universe to touch her, no matter what she was. He seized a flagon from the bar and cracked it against the bartender's temple. The man staggered and threw out an arm that sent a spray of glass shattering. Even as he hit the floor, his eyes rolled up into their sockets.

"Let's go!" urged Alan, gripping the woman's arm.

Voices rang out as they ran for the stage. Chairs screeched against stone. Someone shouted a warning from across the tavern.

But Alan had already followed the woman up a brief set of steps. His boots clicked on stage, inducing the dancing girl to shriek and flee. Or was it something else that alarmed her?

A step ahead of Alan, the tunic-clad woman seized the golden curtain, rippling it like wind-blown water. As she parted it, Alan whirled to the tavern and saw a score of U.S.S. troopers crash through the entrance with drawn Bannings. Before, he had been struck by the woman's air of mystery, but now he was awed. She had known, and warned him.

They fled down a dimly lighted hallway that reeked with sweat. She ran with a lithe, fluid motion that reminded him of a cat, while his own legs quivered with the toll of nine years in the mines.

They hurried past open doorways, saw bare bodies and groping hands, heard girlish giggles and lustful curses. He could taste salt on his lips as weakness overcame him, but on another level he felt strangely powerful, like a boxer looming over a fallen opponent.

The woman reached an open window at hall's end, squeezed through, and dropped into the night. Alan's lungs heaved, expanding and contracting in vicious cycle. By the time he joined her in the alley, he was so exhausted that he collapsed to the refuse-strewn bricks.

She pulled at his arm. "Come on! You've got to come on!"

Alan clawed at the bricks, his nails scraping mud and grime. Then she was helping him, and he regained his feet and looked at her through rain that clouded his eyes.

"Who are you?"

"They'll be here!" She spun to the corner of the building, as if seeing something other than wind-swept trash.

He wanted to collapse again. He wanted to surrender to the screams of his beaten body. Then he remembered the Rayolian Crystal, how he had conquered it with sheer will—and maybe something more—and he found new hope. He would fight! He would conquer the greatest foe of all: that inner voice that cried *No more! No more*!

He ran madly as she gripped his arm. The rain flooded down, as thick as breakers over a schooner. Their feet slapped against brick, splashed through rivulets for so long that his face paled and his vision blackened.

Around the corner of a building in another dark alley, he finally stopped beside boxes of trash soaked by rain. He bent over, hands on knees, feeling his pulse pound inside his head.

"Enough," he gasped. He looked up to find the woman's body perfectly outlined in the soggy tunic as she peered back around the building's edge, checking the alley they had vacated.

She turned, brushing wet hair from her face. "Nobody. We're safe here."

Good enough, thought Alan, but pursuit wasn't his only concern. "Why?" he asked.

She only looked at him.

He wiped his beaded brow with a forearm and nodded to the corner. "Back there in the bar. I don't even know you, yet you warned me, got me out."

She lowered her gaze to the curves of her body. "Maybe we got each other out." She lifted her head again and her eyes took on a distant look, as though she saw something far beyond him. "If it hadn't been for you, he would have killed me."

He frowned and straightened. "Why would he have done that? Aren't you one of his . . ."

He stopped in mid-sentence, embarrassed. He knew what she was, how she had taken men's money and given her body in return. So why did he find it so hard to voice? What strange spark did she ignite in him? What had prompted him to bludgeon a man he had never seen before?

He shook his head. "What I mean is—"

"You know what I am," she interrupted.

"I don't understand about him wanting to kill you, how you knew they were coming." His voice dropped to a hoarse whisper. "I don't understand about . . . Faroul."

The wind turned bitterly cold and she shivered and folded her arms across her breast. "I-I killed a . . ." She spoke as if she found it hard to believe her own words. "A black marketer, he tried to cut me up. I . . ."

Her words faded, her eyes beginning to well, her fingers trembling.

She lowered her gaze. Alan didn't know a thing about this woman, but it didn't dissuade him from putting a compassionate hand on her shoulder.

"It's a rough life in there," he said.

She looked up at him, her face deeply carved.

"Smile," he urged. "A pretty woman like you ought to smile, even if she doesn't want to." He noted the smudged makeup. "I'm Alan Burke."

Her chin quivered, but a thin smile nevertheless lifted the corners of her mouth. "Davon."

He let his gentle hand linger on her shoulder and her smile deepened a little, as if she hadn't known such tenderness in a long time.

"You told me there was danger," he said. "How did you know troops were storming the place?"

"It happened, didn't it?"

"And Faroul. Why would you say that?"

"I . . ." Fright filled her eyes. "All I know is you're going there. *We're going there.*"

The rain trickled down Alan's collar and soaked him to the skin, but the abrupt chill that crawled through his flesh was for another reason, and he didn't know what to say. All he knew was there was solace in her eyes, meaning in her voice.

He took her hand and they walked through the pouring rain toward the northern outskirts of the city.

***

Dawn broke across shifting sands and baked earth with boulders scattered like corpses in a field. The eastern stars faded, swallowed by fiery orange clouds that hugged the horizon like streaming banners. The Zaran sun first appeared through a cleft in distant mountains of rock, and by the time the pair's weary legs carried them to the great spire with scree slope at its base, their own shadows were shortening.

The calluses on Alan's heels had ruptured, and he paused in deference to the raw skin. Davon stopped as well, obviously glad to lift her sandals and shake out the sand.

Alan squinted as he studied the spire silhouetted against a glaring sky. It was a mass of reddish rock, cracked like a decaying building, and it rose a hundred meters to stand against the sun.

"It's here," he said with parched throat. He scanned the surrounding terrain: the volcanic tuffs with wind-hollowed caves, the sand drifts gutted by dry washes. "Somewhere, the craft, crew."

Davon looked as well. "There," she said, pointing.

Still, Alan saw only boulders and piles of rubble. "I don't see it."

Davon started on through sand that crept about her ankles. "Come on."

She brushed past scorched shrubbery, and he studied the distance dictated by her course. No glint of metal, no forward cockpit with jutting nose, just desolation. Maybe the mine dust had robbed his vision, left him half-blind, but then perhaps . . .

He followed after her, and for some reason he could not fathom, he knew she was right.

Beyond the spire in a clearing, concealed by house-sized boulders that had crashed from the cliffs, lay the starship. Sunlight played along the titanium hull, creating a stark contrast with heat shields blackened by re-entry. A hundred meters long and half as high, the ship was imposing, resembling a huge bird with one wing tucked under and the other spread wide. The vessel was not as sophisticated as the enormous carriers that could harbor a hundred fighter craft, but it was similar to the ship with which Alan had wreaked havoc on the U.S.S. fleet for six years.

As he and Davon skirted a great, overhanging megalith, Alan heard a Banning's safety mechanism click off.

"Look out!" he warned, pulling her under the rock.

He whirled skyward, scanning the boulders to the hammer of his heart. Somebody was ready to kill them, no matter the deal Lindsay had struck.

"Here! Up here!" snapped a gruff voice.

Alan spun to the megalith's crest a few meters directly overhead and looked into the muzzle of a Banning. The sights swayed ever so slightly in the grip of a brute-of-a-man backdropped by the towering spire.

A stream of leche juice splattered at Alan's feet. "What the hell you're doin'?" the sentinel demanded.

Alan straightened, his arm growing tighter about Davon. "The same thing you are. Looking for Faroul."

The guard frowned and picked his nose. "The hell you say."

"Juarez. He knows we're coming."

More lemstel juice splattered down. "We'll see about that."

Keeping his Banning on the pair, the pirate scrambled to the ground and nodded to the clearing. "Let's go."

Alan clasped Davon's hand and they walked toward the starship. Two men worked to repair the forward heat shield, their tools glinting in the sunlight. One pirate lay on an elbow, picking his teeth with the point of a gleaming cutlass, while another sat cleaning a Banning, the working parts scattered on a rock beside him. The remainder of the brigands, some brawny with ugly scars and others with skin drawn taut over bones, milled or rested in the dust.

They were a filthy lot: unshaven faces, sweat-streaked brows, dingy trousers and V-necked shirts, fingernails black with grime. There were a dozen or so, consisting of ebony-skinned Thalians, an Oriental, and the rest half-breeds spawned by the slums of three star systems.

Déjà vu came over Alan. He had done this before. He had given up a commission on a carrier, denounced the United Star Systems, vowed vengeance until he died. He had gathered men such as these—outcasts, thieves, political dissenters, deserters—from brothels and black market sectors, filled their minds with greed, gained their respect.

But one day his trust in one of them had led him to the Alosian mines.

Juarez climbed from the starship airlock, and then Lindsay became framed in the hatch.

"Alan!" said the younger man. He dropped to the dust and faced Juarez. "Tell your men he's all right."

Juarez's jaw twitched. "Took you long enough," he snapped to Alan. He nodded to the sentry, who proceeded to holster his weapon.

Juarez approached, gaping at Davon's lithe form and naked legs. "Well, well," he commented, scratching his beard. "Looks like he's done gone and brought us a Thalian whore. Pretty hospitable of him."

Alan's blood ran hot. "Nobody touches her, especially not some pig."

A pirate went for his Banning, but Juarez waved him off. He looked at Lindsay, whose face had turned as pale as a noonday sun. "You better tell your friend to watch his mouth," he snarled. Then he challenged Alan with a glare. "This weak old man don't know what he's liable to get himself into."

Lindsay came to Alan, his eyes imploring silence, cooperation. "I was afraid you didn't make it. Troops, they stormed the place. I hid in a closet and slipped out when I heard Banning fire."

Alan smiled and put a hand on his shoulder. "I was worried about you too, Lin, got scared they might have . . ." His voice faded, swallowed up in emotion.

Lindsay grinned and slapped him playfully on the arm. "Not me. I learned too much from you all those years, about a lot of things." Then his words dropped to a whisper. "I'm sorry for all the things we said back there."

Alan smiled again, remembering how he had held him close as a boy and comforted him, told him about life, its joys and cruelties. "Me too."

He reached for Davon's arm, urging her to his side. "Lin, this is Davon. She's . . ." He looked around and found her eyes meeting his.

Just who was she, after all? What did he know about her, her motives?

It didn't matter. Not after she had warned him, led him to safety when otherwise he would have returned to the mines.

He turned to Lindsay. "She saved my life. She's coming with us."

Lindsay frowned and edged nearer. "Are you serious?" he whispered in disbelief. He motioned to Juarez. "You've got to get along with him, *got to or he'll kill us*. She'll just cause more trouble, more tension."

A strange tingle pierced Alan, and he did not know if it was from fear or anticipation of things beyond his conception. He looked into Davon's face, saw the sunlight turn her hair silky. Why *did* he want to bring her along, this brothel prostitute not unlike hundreds of others?

"Faroul," she had whispered. *Faroul*. There was something about her, some indefinable quality that pricked his mind in a much deeper way than mere curiosity.

He turned to the still-glaring Juarez, framed against the starship. "She goes!" he shouted. "She goes to Faroul, or nobody does!"

Juarez laughed quietly, a laugh filled with contempt and something worse. "That's fine with me." He looked at his crew. "Fine with *all* of us, now ain't it, guys?"

A dozen pirates grinned and laughed lecherously.

Chapter Seven

Davon sat alone in her quarters, listening to the hum of the air jets supporting the mattress beneath her. Her stomach churned, and she looked down at her palms, remembering how blood had filled the lines.

How could she have done it? How could she have driven a dagger into the chest of a living person, no matter what he was?

She glanced at her breasts and slim hips and remembered the hundreds of men, how she had smiled seductively and fluffed back her hair to make her figure more pronounced, more irresistible. The black marketer hadn't been the first who had sought sexual satisfaction by doing her physical harm; there had been others just as bad, worse. So why this time had she so rebelled? Why had she been so filled with desire to escape her sordid lifestyle that she had killed him?

The brightness of the light above caught her attention, and the eerie vision came back. Vague images, like a distant red glow through dense fog. A strong man with will and perseverance, and she at his side, beyond the ages.

No, it couldn't be. Alan was too weather-beaten, too broken in body. But his spirit . . . That was what had obsessed her from the moment she had first seen him in vision years ago, and ultimately had made her ashamed of what she was.

Perplexed, she dwelled on the mysteries that had always enveloped her life.

She was four years old in Zaran years, and the mountain air was crisp. Sitting in her mother's lap on the open roof of a stone cottage, she listened to the rustle of the coloring book in her tiny hands. A few meters away lay a wall and then precipice, for like other edifices in this remote village, their home was built into a high bluff overlooking a rocky stream. Her older sister giggled as she played along the roof, the wind tousling her curly blonde hair as sunlight glinted from her golden necklace.

Davon felt her mother gently rock her in her arms. She could smell the freshness of her hair, like clothes dried in sunshine. In the distance a bird sang happily, and Davon looked down at the picture of wings in flight that had occupied her efforts.

Suddenly she no longer wanted to color a bird. She yearned for a picture of her own. She flipped the pages with childish eagerness and began to draw. A line here, a curve there. It consumed her young mind passionately, obsessing her as nothing else ever had.

Her mother evidently noticed and brushed a hand across her daughter's cheek. "What in the world are you drawing, Davon? Here, let me see." She took the book and started to glance at it.

"Look, Mama!" cried Davon's sister. "Look at me!"

As her mother obliged, Davon felt an abrupt tremor grip the usually comforting arms.

"Shannon!" The woman set Davon aside and leaped up in a panic. "Shannon! Get down!"

The girl was atop the wall, walking it with arms tilted like glider wings. "See, Mama," she said, showing off as the wind whipped her blonde curls. "I told you I could, Mama."

"No!" The woman dropped the book in her frantic rush across the roof. "No, Shannon, no!"

"I told you I could, Mama," said the little girl, laughing, her bare feet hugging the narrow ledge. "I—"

A sudden gust. Arms flailing wildly. A toe slipping free, then a foot.

"Mama! *Help me, Mama! Mammaaa!*"

Then came a long, horrible scream that grew fainter and fainter until it died in the mother's cries.

The woman collapsed across the top of the wall, her long hair cascading toward the roaring stream below. Davon, not understanding but suddenly very afraid, felt the air turn viciously cold as she ran to her.

"Mama? What's wrong, Mama? Where's Shannon?"

Her mother sobbed loudly and turned, pulling her so close that Davon could feel the tears against her cheek. What was wrong? Why was she crying? She had never seen her mother this way, had never felt so afraid.

The wind rustled the coloring book, lying a meter away. The pages flipped one at a time, and then dozens at once, coming to rest on the page where Davon had drawn the picture. Through eyes blurred by grief, the woman looked at it and an even greater shudder seized her.

There, scrawled in childish images, was the unmistakable picture of a woman leaning over a cliff.

And far below, crushed against rocks alongside a stream, lay the body of a girl.

A knock on the door startled Davon back to the present.

"Davon? It's me, Alan. Can I come in?"

She straightened, brushing the moisture from her cheeks and trying to control her emotions. "Just . . . Just a minute."

She smoothed out her tunic, pressed a button at the head of the bed, and the door slid open, framing Alan in the threshold. He had shaven and combed his gray-streaked hair, and the clothes that the gritty desert winds had soiled were freshly laundered. In his hands was a green flight uniform.

He nodded to it. "Thought you might want to put this on."

"Come on in," she said, rising.

He crossed the cabin and the door slid shut. He stopped before her, his eyes seeming to wander to her almost-bare shoulders. Looking up, he handed her the uniform. "Here," he said. "Maybe with this on you won't look so much like . . ." His voice faded. "We've got a ship full of pirates who can't even begin to know what a woman's all about."

She was surprised at his sensitivity. "I can't understand you. One moment you seem so filled with anger, and the next . . ."

He shrugged. "You know, I never did get around to thanking you for getting me out of that bar. You'd never even *seen* me before. That's what I can't figure out."

She looked directly into his eyes. "I don't know the reason *you* did the things you did. Why you hit the bartender, followed me, stood up for me outside the ship. And then insisting I be brought along when you didn't even know me."

"You didn't know me either." The air jets hummed for long seconds. "I guess there's something about you that made me trust you."

She took his hand, nodded to the mattress. "Let's talk."

He hesitated. "No," he said, glancing at the bed. "It's been too long, too many years in the mines."

Davon felt a rush of blood to her cheeks and she withdrew her hand. "That's not what I meant," she snapped, lifting her head defiantly. "You think that's all I am, all I want from life? One minute you defend me, tell me how all those others can't understand, then here you are thinking I just want to use you, let you use me."

He drew back, evidently surprised and embarrassed. "I'm sorry," he said, almost in a whisper. "I . . . didn't mean to say anything to hurt you, sorry I took it wrong. My head's not as clear as it used to be. You don't know what it's like to lay in your own vomit and let the rats gnaw on you for nine years."

Again she took his hand, this time with empathy. "Then tell me, who you are, what you've been through."

He studied her for long seconds before nodding to the bed. "Let's sit," he said quietly.

They eased down, the air jets laboring quietly in support. With the change in position, the slits in her tunic rose to mid-thigh, but now his focus was elsewhere.

"You want to know who *I* think I am, or what others think?" he asked.

"Whatever you feel like telling me."

"Everybody else thinks I'm a traitor who turned against his own empire, as if it was worth holding allegiance to in the first place. They're right about one thing. There's the United Star Systems, and then there's me. That's as simple as I can put it. I'll either destroy it or see it destroy me."

"Why?" she pressed. "What do you hate about it so?"

The loathing swept over his face. "Growing up on Rhythia, my father taught me a lot of things . . . the value of love and forgiveness, that there was nothing nobler than peace and learning how to live together. Whenever I got mad at someone, swore I'd pay them back, he'd take me in his arms and tell me to forgive, pray for them.

"He was the finest man I've ever known, always helping anyone who asked. He'd loan credits he knew he'd never see again, lived his life praying for everybody that mistreated him."

His words faded, and for a long while there was only silence.

"He must have been a wonderful person, to do all that," said Davon.

Alan's cheek twitched. "He was a fool."

She frowned, not understanding.

His eyes narrowed. "Nobody ever cared, appreciated a thing he did. They played him for a fool and laughed behind his back. It was the same way with the U.S.S. He loved the empire. He worked his guts out in the Rhythian parliament trying to help the U.S.S. civilize the planet, get the people out of their poverty.

"He got me believing so strongly in the cause that when I turned eighteen I joined the Galactic Patrol, got a commission on a starship carrier. Then the Great Insurrection broke out. You know the story. The rebels tried to overthrow the government and gathered so much support that the U.S.S. decided to stop them, no matter the cost.

"We were ordered to trail them, all the way across two solar systems. Then our informants told us they were hiding on Rhythia, right where I was raised. You know what we were ordered to do? We launched a hundred fighter craft. They razed the planet, killed millions of innocent people, left it in rubble. My father was one of them. I looked out the porthole and watched a thousand nuclear missiles destroy his world."

Davon swallowed hard, feeling in a small way the grief he felt, and placed a caring hand on his shoulder. "I-I'm sorry, Alan, sorry I made you tell me, sorry it happened."

He clenched his teeth. "I sabotaged the computers, took a fighter craft, deserted, swore I'd destroy the whole empire for what they'd done."

"Your bitterness," she said. "I understand the reason, but you can't let it rule your life."

He ignored her. "I dropped out to the slums of the colonies, drank my way out of depression, forgot the nuclear warheads in the lemstel. I began rounding up cutthroats and scoundrels, all the outcasts of the colonies, became a pirate. We'd attack incoming freighters loaded with military supplies, take the booty and destroy them. For six years we eluded the empire, striking here and there, hitting them where it hurt worst."

He nodded to the doorway. "Lindsay. He was just a boy, headed to the colonies with his family. Their transport accidentally crossed into a forbidden zone and a military starship attacked it. They killed everybody except a frightened little boy that I took on board and raised like my own son.

"My crew was the lowest scum in the galaxy. Except for Lin, there was only one I placed any trust in, a lifelong pirate named Poteet. One day we attacked a military transport, disabled it, found a top-secret prisoner on board. Kasterfayette. I thought he was just a dying old man, but I took him in and laid him in my quarters, listened to a strange story about a place he called Faroul.

"Poteet listened long enough to let his greed take control. I sent him out, didn't let him hear the details of the old man's story or the way to get there. That's why he sold me out to the United Star Systems, led me to a trap in a lemstel dive, caused me to lose nine years of my life on Alos."

"Faroul," she said quietly, and the word seemed to echo through the cabin. "What do you know about it?"

He stiffened. "Maybe I should ask you the same thing."

She felt herself flush again, and dropped her gaze. "I can't explain what I don't understand myself. It's like a long road leading down a hill, an intersection here, a pathway there, a multitude of streets stretched out like a maze. It's as if sometimes down a certain route I can make out images, faces, events, as if I'm seeing a dim light through falling rain."

"You're not making sense."

"I didn't say it made sense. All I know is last night, just like my whole life long, I caught a glimpse of someone like you, myself, and a place . . ." Squinting, she put her hand to her temple. "No, an event, an occurrence, that is Faroul."

Alan laughed nervously. "Right here in the age of interstellar travel, and you've brought goose bumps all over me from a silly dream you had."

"No," she snapped. "It's not silly. It's Faroul, and we're going there. You'll follow a road like Blake Sharrel's, a shadow path alongside his."

"Like whose?" asked Alan. "Wasn't he the one that got through the Violeshan Web just before all the great wars broke out, after a thousand years without any? The one that disappeared in deep space with some archaeologist, Rhonda Gregory, I think her name was?"* [*See *Starflight to Destiny* by Patrick Dearen.]

"You're in his shadow path already," said Davon. "It's carrying you along, making you experience some of the things he did. When you're far enough down it, your path will go off on its own. It's the only way for you to get to Faroul."

Alan shrank back and stood. "It's mad, crazy, as crazy as Kasterfayette's story." He walked away a few steps, rubbing his face, and then looked back at her. "Everybody respected Kasterfayette. His books on nuclear energy and cosmology were studied in every university. But he got mixed up in religion, Mideast archaeology on Earth, claimed he'd uncovered ancient Hebrew manuscripts around the Dead Sea.

"He got the crazy idea that those scrolls pinpointed a place in the galaxy—Faroul, he called it—where creation would occur, once a certain key unlocked the mysteries. Even the religious fanatics laughed at him. But he got obsessed with it, went around trying to drum up monetary support for a mission there till finally he got a few followers.

"He was like a prophet to them, and they built a whole new pseudoscientific religion out of meaningless Bible passages that talk about a new heaven and Earth being created."

Davon stood and came nearer. "It doesn't sound like you believe much in the Bible."

He shrugged. "Why should I? Sure, I studied Hebrew. My father drilled it into me. But look where his faith got him." He lowered his head and stared at his shin-high black boots, and then looked up at her. "Kasterfayette and his followers stole a starship, disappeared out into the galaxy. He came back alone, a withered old man, beaten and broken.

"And you know what? The U.S.S., which believes technology can destroy anything that stands in its way, was so afraid of the legend, so scared of what he might know, they tried to brainwash him, sap him of all his knowledge.

"They couldn't—he must've been quite a man—yet the U.S.S. never gave up hope of wringing Faroul's location out of him. They were transporting him to Alos, figuring the Rayolian Crystal would rob him of his will, when we attacked the starship.

"I took him to my cabin, and with his dying breaths he talked about Faroul. He told me about a decaying wall with Hebraic inscriptions, how he had held the secret of creation in his hands, but lost it. After I ordered Poteet out, Kasterfayette pulled me close and whispered its location."

She put a hand to her temple again. "But what can all that mean?"

He laughed lowly and nodded in the direction of the forward control room. "They think it means whoever makes it there will be like a god and learn to create, just like Poteet believes." He shook his head skeptically. "Legend, just silly legend."

She studied his face intently. "Is that everything you know about Faroul?"

He looked away as if his vision was shrouded by mystery, confusion.

"All I care about is destroying the U.S.S.," he said.

He went to the door and the sensor automatically opened it.

"Alan."

He turned and looked back.

"Your father," she said quietly. "You're wrong. He wasn't a fool."

Alan merely walked out the door, but Davon wondered if her words went with him.

Chapter Eight

"All right, you're the one that knows the way to Faroul, so what are the coordinates?"

Juarez stood in the passageway beside the spiral stairs that led upward to the navigational section and glared at Alan as Lindsay stood watching. They had just left orbit about Zara II, and Alan noted how the pirate's eyes already burned with anticipation and greed. He turned to Lindsay.

"I thought we were going after Poteet." He nodded to Juarez. "Doesn't he know?"

Lindsay paled, his lips trembling.

"What are you trying to pull?" Juarez demanded of Alan, his eyes suddenly savage. "That little wimp promised us Faroul. We made a deal, and by God you're going to carry it out or I'll kill you both."

Alan looked at how the corridor lights reflected from Lindsay's cheekbone. "You better tell me something, Lin. You better tell *him* something."

Lindsay shifted his eyes nervously from one to the other before facing the pirate. "But Poteet, we—"

Juarez clutched Lindsay's collar, jerking him to his beard. "I don't give a damn about Poteet. You better have him give me those coordinates or you'll wish you'd've never got out of that whorehouse."

Alan's blood surged. He slammed the heel of his hand against Juarez's shoulder, shoving him back. The pirate withdrew from Lindsay and went for his Banning, his eyes colder than ever.

"No!" yelled Lindsay. He was between the two, imploring cooperation. "You kill him and you'll never get to Faroul! Never!"

Juarez's fingers slowly relaxed on his holster, but he lifted a threatening fist toward Alan. "I may need you, all right, but I don't figure we need that whore you seem so crazy about."

The pirate was posturing, and Alan knew it. "Don't threaten me," he said. "You so much as lay a hand on her and I'll kill you. Now, Lindsay promised you Faroul. Okay, then that's just what you're going to get. But first we've got some business to take care of with Poteet. You said the last you heard he was working the Myolian system. If he's still there we've got a clear road to Faroul. If he's not, if he knows the way and is already halfway there, then we damned sure better know, because he'll put up a hell of a fight to keep it all to himself."

"Can't we just assume he's on his way?" spoke up Lindsay. "Why waste time?"

"Finding out if we're ripe for ambush is time well-spent," defended Alan. Then he glared at Juarez. "Those are my terms, or Faroul's secret dies with me."

Juarez sucked in air through broken teeth. He rasped a hand across his bristly face, and then turned and went up the stairway.

As the report of the pirate's boots died away, Lindsay confronted Alan. "My Lord, don't you have any sense left? He could kill you, kill us both anytime he gets ready."

Alan stared at the metal steps winding upward and smiled faintly. "I know. But he won't. He values his greed too highly, values what I know."

Lindsay looked down at the floor and shook his head. "I just don't know about you anymore. I can't understand why you think nobody can hurt you."

"I've been in hell nine years. Could anything be worse?"

Lindsay started away, but hesitated. "Faroul. You've never told anyone else where it's at, not even me."

"There's something strange about all this, Lin, a couple of things I can't quite figure out."

"What's that?"

"If Poteet overheard what Kasterfayette told me, if he knows Faroul's whereabouts, then why'd he wait nine years to go after it?"

Lindsay shrugged. "How should I know?" Wheeling, he started away again, the legs of his flight uniform rasping against one another.

"There's something else that bothers me, Lin."

The younger man paused and turned.

Alan looked directly into his face. "I can't quite figure out how you pulled off my escape, how you just happened to be there when I decided to make my break."

"That's easy. I spent five months there, watching you every day, asking questions. That guard you killed, he'd told me that day that there was something different about you, something defiant. So I watched you, suggested you carry the body to the pit. It wasn't the first time I'd looked for a way to spring you."

Alan stood staring at him for long seconds, weighing every detail of his account. It made sense enough, he supposed, as much sense as the light in his cell, his defeat of the crystal, his survival in the mines.

He smiled. "I'm glad you were there, Lin, glad it was you."

The younger man smiled in return and walked away.

***

The first few days out of Thalia were uneventful. Alan rested, downed hundreds of vitamins, partook heartily of the artificially manufactured food, and exercised in his cabin. At first, as he stood bathing in the Catholian Ray and viewed his reflection in the booth, he could hardly believe that the mines had sapped his body so. He was an emaciated old man who reminded him strangely of Kasterfayette: ribs like fence posts, tired eyes, skin drawn tightly over arms and legs.

But as the ship's chronometer registered days and then a week, he began to notice subtle changes. He felt himself growing stronger, the muscles in his legs hardening, his breathing stabilizing. At times he would still break out coughing horribly; the mine dust had forever left its imprint in his lungs. But at least he found security in knowing that with each passing day, he was becoming more of a human being again.

He was allowed freedom to roam the ship, other than the section where the main computers lay. He spent much of his time on the forward control deck, where stars sped toward him from open space like reflections whirling in a dark pool.

Juarez showed open hostility through physical nuances, but the other pirates seemed to accept the presence of outsiders. They tolerated and went about their duties, checking instruments, inventorying booty from a ransacked freighter and dividing it.

But tensions mounted.

They sat about a long table in the commissary: a survivor of Alos, an escapee from the Thalian brothels, a former U.S.S. guard, and several pirates, thieves, and lemstel addicts. It was meal time, and the odor of food produced from raw chemicals permeated the air. Silverware clanged against platter; corsairs guzzled lemstel from flagons; liquid dribbled down chins and moistened tangled beards. They tore at meat savagely, ripping out hunks with their teeth, and wiped greasy hands on thighs.

Alan sat flanked by Davon and Lindsay and tried to ignore the suggestive conversation led by Juarez at the head of the table. It was difficult, because the pirate delighted in detailing his last encounter with a slum prostitute, and more than once Alan caught him looking at how tightly the flight uniform hugged Davon's breasts.

A swarthy Thalian with a scar on his brow wiped his mouth with his hand and interrupted Juarez. "Enough of your whorin'," he said. "Those crates of jewels we took off that last freighter . . ."

The Thalian suddenly seemed to realize he had overstepped his bounds. Glancing around, he found every flagon in limbo and all eyes fixed on him: the cold and the narrow, the glazed and the expectant.

Juarez reached for another steak and never looked up. "What about it?" With such a large bite in his mouth, the words barely were distinguishable.

The Thalian looked about the table. Sweat trickled down his forehead and glistened in the deck lights. No one moved, spoke.

He looked back at Juarez and watched him tear into meat, his lips smacking and the front of his V-necked shirt growing wet with grease. "We counted it all today," said the Thalian, his every word like the tick of a bomb. "Those crates. When we first took them aboard they were full. Now . . ." He surveyed the other pirates again, as if looking for support, encouragement. And found only stares.

He spun to Juarez. "The jewels. They're missing, A bunch of 'em. I saw them myself, carried 'em to the freight bay. Now they're gone."

Juarez took a long, hard drink of lemstel and left a stream down his chin. "Well, then, maybe *you're* the one knows where they're at," he commented, eyes still fixed on his food.

The Thalian grated his chair back and jumped to his feet. "You damned right I do! I looked in your cabin and found ever' last one of 'em."

Everyone stiffened as if a hot iron had thrust against ribs. Davon edged nearer Alan. Juarez was caught in mid-bite, and as he looked up over oily hands and steak, his eyes were as cold as shadows in deep space.

He slowly lowered his food. "So you're saying *what*?" he demanded. He scooted back his chair, rose to his full height as his hairy belly showed through a crease in his shirt. The Banning dangling loosely at his hip took on an ominous presence.

The Thalian slung an accusing finger at him. "I'm saying *you* took it! And it's not the first time. We risk our necks, then you steal it right out from under our noses!" He pivoted to his companions. "All of you know it. You know it and don't have the guts to stand up to him!" He turned to Juarez again and gritted his teeth. "No more! You're not taking no more credits of mine!"

Juarez laughed lowly, a laugh that chilled Alan. He reached for Davon's hand beneath the table, closing on her fingers, wishing for a Banning. He had seen similar situations on his own ship: greed overcame fear, emotions trampled trust born of respect, and violence became the by-product.

"You know," said Juarez, wiping his mouth with his sleeve, "if it was you that brought those jewels on board, you that discovered 'em missing, you that supposedly found 'em . . ." He surveyed the pirates and nodded to the Thalian. "Seems to me, all you scum, *he's* the thief around here. You're sitting here eating, and he's stealing your credits and laughing at you."

"You filthy liar!" growled the Thalian. He whirled to the others. "You know him, know what he is! We can take him. We can take him now! Just stand up and fight for yourselves for once!"

Alan felt a tremor grip Davon.

Juarez grinned smugly and studied the cutthroats at the table. "Well?" he asked. He motioned to the Thalian. "He called me a lying thief." He paused, letting the drama build. "I say *he's* the one taking booty, when all the rest of you do the dirty work, the killing and plundering. So just who you figure on believing?"

A grim stillness pervaded the table, like a rodent motionless a strike's distance from a cobra. Alan surveyed the corsairs, sensed the multitude of thoughts in the craggy faces. He knew what the potbellied man with acne-scarred cheeks was going to say even before the pale lips began to move.

"You've always treated us fair, Juarez," he said.

"No!" cried the Thalian, turning on his comrade. "Tell the truth! You know!"

"We're behind you, Juarez!" spoke up a yellow-bearded man beyond Lindsay.

As though they were one, the remaining pirates shouted their agreement.

"You're fools!" yelled the Thalian. "All of you, you're fools!"

Juarez grinned broadly, revealing jagged teeth. "You know what we do with thieves, don't you?" he said to the men. "With thieves that try to take more than their share?"

The Thalian went for his Banning. Chairs screeched back and overturned. From behind the Thalian, arms restrained him, cruel, merciless arms.

"Kill him!" someone cried from Alan's left. "Kill the thief!"

A cutlass flashed up, gleaming in the light. Curses. Struggle. Cries. And blood abruptly streaming down the Thalian's spine like water from a severed pipe.

Davon gasped.

"Let's get out of here!" said Alan, pulling her from the table and rushing for the doorway.

He glanced around just as the door slid shut behind them, and suddenly realized whose voice it had been that had cried out from his left, whose pronouncement of sentence had preceded the thrust of the cutlass.

It had been Lindsay's.

Chapter Nine

In Davon's cabin, Alan stood with his arms about her and tried to soothe her tremor as she laid her head against his shoulder. He could smell the fragrance of her perfume, the fresh scent of her hair. The touch of her skin sent a tingle through his frame, arousing long-submerged memories and desires.

Her soft sobs left wetness against his neck. "It's okay, Davon," he said quietly. "You're here with me. Nobody's going to hurt you."

She looked up into his eyes. For the first time Alan saw how much loneliness they held, how much they seemed to reach out for comfort. "Why did they do it?" she asked. "They knew he was telling the truth, knew Juarez was lying."

"I know. But they're out here in deep space, wanted by every authority in the colonies. Juarez, they have to trust him, have to trust someone to keep them alive. It's trust based on fear, like a wolf pack with one leader. The strongest leads and the others follow. And survive.

"Where the Thalian made his mistake was not challenging Juarez to a fight in the airlock. That's how pirate crews decide the strongest."

"Is that the way it was with you? You led your crew and attacked all those freighters because they were afraid of you?"

"That's part of it. Fear breeds respect." He nodded to the secured door. "It also breeds hatred, like out there a while ago. They all hate Juarez's guts, know he steals, lies like a dog. But they also know he keeps them alive, leads them to more booty. That's why he stands out there and laughs while the Thalian gets a blade in his back. He knows he's the strongest, most capable, and the rest know it too."

Davon buried her face into the nape of his neck. "I thought if I could just get away from that place, get away from the slums, I'd be free of all this." She quaked, and he held her tighter, suddenly as in need of her comforting arms as she was of his. "All my life I've been so alone. Nobody knows what it's like when even your own mother doesn't care, leaves you to die."

Alan ran his hand lightly over her hair, feeling the silky texture. "Was that how it was? Don't think about it. Just remember I'm here with you now and you're not alone. Not anymore, because I need you."

She slowly looked up, questions in her features. Her hands played along his shoulders, back of his neck. "Do you really mean that?" she whispered. "You know what I am, how many men . . ." Her lips began to tremble.

He smiled and pulled her close. "I said so, didn't I?" He bent nearer her face, his fingers gentle along her cheek, and then his mouth became tender against hers.

They stayed entwined in each other's arms for a long while, the warmth of her body stirring primeval urges inside Alan. Then Davon withdrew, only to place her head against his chest.

"I'm worried," she said, "just so worried."

"What about? I told you I'm here."

She looked into his face again. "That makes me happy. *You* make me happy. But . . ." She ran her hand lightly along his upper arm. "It's Juarez. He wants me, and sooner or later he's going to do something about it."

Alan squeezed her hand. "Not while I'm around," he said angrily. "Not while Lindsay . . ."

He started, again struck by Lindsay's cry in the commissary. He looked away, the room fading, and disengaged his arms from her.

"Alan? What's wrong?"

He shook his head, trying to understand. "I don't know. There's something not right, something that doesn't make sense."

Her hands were gentle on his shoulder. "It's Lindsay, isn't it? It's Lindsay you're worried about, unsure of."

He turned to stare into her face and didn't know what to say.

***

Five chronological days later, at the midway point on the journey to the Myolian system, Davon descended to the lowest level of the craft and sought solitude before the porthole in the shadows of the freight bay.

She had to think, had to thrash things out. She pressed her face against the glass, feeling the coolness, and stared into space. She had never been on a spacecraft before and she felt overwhelmed when she considered the pinpoints of light in infinite blackness, the swirls of the galaxy looming like slender clouds. It was like a veil out there, a dark veil hiding planets, stars, galaxies, galactic clusters. And the mysteries of her life.

There was something frightening about the jewel-like stars that blurred in her vision, a mystical quality about the way she stood alone watching the universe recede from her, leaving utter darkness, cold and demonic, in its wake, like that long-ago day when the midday sun seemed not to exist.

"Davon, Davon, daughter of a demon!" chanted the children, circling her with arms joined. *"Drew her picture, falling, fallen!"*

She lay in the dust with skinned knee, scraped elbow, and watched them dance about her, stirring clouds of dirt with each step. She was crying, wanting them to stop, wishing her mother would come for her.

"Davon, Davon, daughter of a demon!"

"No!" she screamed in her girlish voice. "He was an angel! An angel!"

"Well, well," said a caustic voice from the shadows, "if it's not the Thalian whore."

Davon started, whirling from the porthole. Crates and food cylinders were stacked in piles, leaving dark, sinister canyons yawning between. Her heart began to pummel, for there was shadow within one of the shadows: the silhouette of a bearded man coming nearer.

"What do you want?" she blurted.

Quiet laughter pervaded the bay, laughter that she recognized as Juarez's, and it sent fear racing through her. *Got to get away! Got to run!*

She tried to retreat, but the frigid porthole pressed into her shoulder blades.

Juarez rubbed his nose and grinned broadly as he came closer, framed between bundles of supplies. "You know," he said, smacking his lips, "I hear tell you Thalian whores are just about the best there is."

"Go to hell," she snapped.

He laughed again. "You know something? I can have anything on this ship—you included—and there's not anybody that can do a thing about it."

She spun about like a cornered animal, searching for escape. She ran, crashed against boxes, overturned them like dominoes, lost her balance. Slamming into the floor, she looked up to find him standing above, a cruel smile on his lips and lust in his eyes.

"What's the matter with you?" he snarled. "I bet you never ran like that back in that whorehouse." He laughed again, his hairy belly rolling like cresting waves. "I bet you kinda liked it, didn't you?"

Davon turned to claw at the floor, her screams dying in the mysteries of space.

Chapter Ten

She was alone. She lay sobbing quietly beside the overturned boxes in the darkness and she was alone.

Her elbow ached as she sat up. With trembling fingers she dressed, feeling the texture of the uniform, the smoothness of the metal buttons. She came to her knees, the rivets in the floor hard beneath her, and tried to stifle her sobs.

Putting her hand to her eyes, she remembered. The dimly lighted backrooms of a dozen Thalian brothels. The palaces of delight where for a few credits a man could live any of his fantasies, could possess her body until he tired of it and tossed it away like an empty keg. She remembered the smell of yellow-stained teeth and sweat-streaked skin in her face, her hands on hundreds of bare backs as arms pawed away at her.

So what was so different this time, and on that night she had killed the man? What was it that had made her loathe the groping arms, forced lips, sweaty bodies ever since she had looked into the light and been sure of Alan and Faroul?

Hatred kindled inside her. Hatred at herself, at Juarez for subjecting her to such an abominable act. She would see him dead! She would see him castrated, mutilated. The bastard, he would die!

She came to her feet, straightening her hair. Alan! She would go to him, tell him what had happened, and he would—

She started. A great pain pierced her forehead, and she brushed her hand across her brow. She turned to the infinity through the porthole, sensing the loneliness out there, the helplessness within her.

She pressed her head against the glass and watched moisture form on it like tiny silver beads. She couldn't. She remembered the scene in the dining hall, the blade thrusting in and out like a Zaran trombone dripping with blood.

She couldn't! She thought of Alan's anger, his penchant for vengeance. He would confront Juarez, try to slay him, and Juarez would stand and laugh as his men slit Alan's throat.

Oh, Alan! She must keep it inside her, hide the truth and go on as though nothing had happened. She would have to let the filthy swine come to her and do it again and again.

The galactic clusters seemed to eddy, like water beneath falls. They took shape, forming images that flooded her mind: images of herself, Alan, and another in Faroul, the power of creation a flaming shield before them.

Alan! Help me!

The only reply was the sound of her own sobs.

***

Alan walked the corridors of the starship alone and remembered.

He remembered the time—eons ago, it seemed now—when his left leg didn't drag slightly, when he could straighten his fingers, when he could inhale deeply without feeling a sharp twinge in his lungs.

He remembered also how he had gained the respect of a savage band of corsairs motivated by greed—greed and lust, much the same as those men who brushed past in the navigation room, who eyed him at meal time as if he were a strange dog.

He had always denied his men the women who had worn the empire's double-eagle insignia, but he had never failed to give them their fair share of confiscated goods. He had let them enjoy the fruits of their piracy until their pockets spilled over with the jewels of the colonies. And he would sit staring at star charts plotting the next assault, and find momentary satisfaction in knowing that he alone carried on a last-ditch fight against the U.S.S.

He cursed. He had never known when to be satisfied, when to back off. Every time he had considered it, his father's image had burned in his mind, the peace-loving father who had believed in the empire and who had died because of it.

And now, the U.S.S. had forever left its mark on his own body, every cough and halting step a stark reminder.

He hated them! For what they had done to his father! For what they had done to himself!

He stared down at the reflection in his boots, lost in his dreams and frustrations as he negotiated a corner. He heard other footsteps, glimpsed Davon's oncoming form too late to avoid a collision.

He caught her by the shoulders as she recoiled.

"Alan! You scared me!"

He relaxed his tensed hands, but let his fingers linger on her upper arms. The air from the vent above swept through her hair like waves lapping a peaceful beach.

He smiled. "I just about jumped out of these boots myself."

"I . . ." She lowered her gaze.

Alan sensed an unease about her. "Hey, what's wrong? Davon? Come on, smile for me."

She looked up, and only now did he notice the wetness in her reddened eyes. "You going to tell me what's wrong?" he pressed. "I may not have known you long, but I can tell *something's* bothering you."

"I . . . I was just walking, thinking." She shook her head. "What do you think of me, Alan? As a woman, a person?"

He studied her with concern, not knowing how to answer. She disengaged herself from his arms and turned away, quietly sobbing.

Perplexed, Alan went to her, sensing that she needed him more than ever before, that he needed her. From behind, he placed tender hands on her shoulders. "Davon, I—"

She spun, her face strained. "You know what I am!" she exclaimed. "A whore, a filthy Thalian whore! I went out, twisted my hips, threw my shoulders back to make my breasts look bigger. I'd take their credits, smile, and claw at their backs while they grunted and groaned and did anything they wanted. I lost myself in all the filth and disease and stopped caring. Then you had to come along, make me look at myself, see me for what I was. Why couldn't you have just left me alone, let me die there?"

Alan was taken aback. "I . . ." He shook his head. "Davon, it was you that got *me* out of there. I never asked you to, never made you go with me."

She looked away, her hand covering her eyes. "You don't understand," she sobbed. "If I hadn't seen you, hadn't seen Faroul, I could've lived with myself. But you made me ashamed of everything I'd become."

He put his hand on her cheek. "I don't know much about you, Davon, the circumstances that led you to that place, but I do know one thing." He paused, and she turned to him. "You're somebody I care about, somebody I hope cares about me. It doesn't make any difference to me what you've been or done. All that matters is what you are now and what you're going to be."

She looked at him for long seconds, her features unmoved, but then more emotions surfaced. "I never thought I'd hear anyone say that, never thought anybody could understand. Nobody knows the emptiness when you're the only one in the world, when there's nobody to fall back on. All my life it's been that way, even when I was little, in the village in the mountains. I never fit in. The other children called me names.

Nobody would have anything to do with me. They were scared of me, even my own mother. She . . ."

The words died like a voice across storm-tossed waters.

"Davon, why would they have been afraid of you?"

"Because," she whispered, "I saw things before they happened, because my father . . ." She seized his arms, the nails digging in. *The stars, Alan. He came from the stars.*"

"What are you talking about? We *all* come from one star system or another, Zara, Sol, Myolia."

She shook her head adamantly. "No. I said from the *stars*"—she nodded upward—"from out there, the galaxy, the heavens."

"You're not making sense."

"I know it doesn't make sense. Nothing does, not me, not Faroul, not even you. All I know is what my mother told me."

She pulled away and breathed sharply. *"Mother!"* she said with contempt. "All she ever did for me was lie to them when I needed her most, just because she was afraid of what they'd do to her."

Her eyes took on a misty, faraway look. "I finally begged her to tell me. Missionaries lived in the village with us, and she told me how she once went off up in the mountains by herself to pray and study the Bible. I'll never forget the way her voice trembled when she told me how she was reading by firelight, how the wind caught the pages, flipped them to Genesis.

"She said her eyes fell on the sixth chapter: 'The sons of God came in to the daughters of men, and they bore children to them. These were the mighty men that were of old, the men of renown.'

"Then somebody came out of the forest, scared her, a young man she didn't know. She jumped up to run, but he told her not to be afraid, that he was there to fulfill that story."

When she placed quivering fingers on Alan's arm, he felt a sudden coldness, like a blizzard on a gloomy night.

"When I was born," she continued, "everybody thought I was a witch, that my father was a demon. When I was older they cast me out, stoned me, left me to die. Even my own mother spit in my face."

"I . . ." Alan didn't know how to respond. "Stories," he finally managed in a hoarse whisper. "Stories and silly legends."

She sobbed and he pulled her close. "It'll be okay, Davon. Don't cry, please don't."

He abruptly became intensely aware of the pounding of his blood, and remembered the mysterious look in her eyes when she had leaned close to him in the Rogues' Tavern and whispered . . .

. . . *Faroul!*

And he did not know what was legend and what was reality.

***

The ship sped on through deep space between star systems, crossing the void that contained only micrometeoroids that pelted the shields, and clouds of dust that veiled distant star clusters which seemed to twirl like sunlight in running water. Soon Myolia, a small sun with three planets in its grasp, loomed like a crystalline orb, a stark contrast to the boundless emptiness that encased it.

Alan stood at the porthole in his quarters and stared, sensing how immensely alone Myolia and its tiny planets really were. They lay before him, neither floating nor supported. They were just there. And far in the opposite direction, had he been able to see it, was the mere pinpoint of light that was its nearest companion, Zara.

A speck here, a speck there. In the same way that electrons whirled about a nucleus, planets whirled about a star, and stars about a gravitational center in a cluster. Star clusters, in turn, whirled about a galactic center, and groups of galaxies about their own centers.

And he, a grain of sand before a vast, mysterious ocean, alone and crying out for someone.

All the events had brought back the questions that had haunted him years before. What was he doing here, a small dot among infinity? Why had he been placed within it when it was far beyond his capabilities ever to affect any of that vastness in even an infinitesimal way?

He thought of his father, felt his arms about him, saw him smile and tousle his hair. *"It's too wonderful, this knowledge, too lofty for me to obtain, how He created all of this by His spoken word, how He will create a new heaven and Earth."*

Alan looked into the black expanse and for a moment he thought he could see a light, warm and solacing, indwelling him with a destiny of his own.

Chapter Eleven

The starship had been within the gravitational pull of Myolia a few hours when Alan climbed into the forward control deck and faced the heavens through the sweeping porthole that formed a hood on three sides.

Computers chimed with almost musical qualities. A thin black man sat at the navigator's post and other crewmen studied instrument readouts. Lindsay and Juarez stood framed against constellations on the left. As Alan approached he could not help but notice how attentive Lin seemed, how all his senses seemed eager to lap up anything the pirate leader had to say.

It brought back memories of a time when Lin had so stood before himself. But no, he was just imagining it all; he still thought of Lin as the boy under his wing. He was grown now, and had enough experiences behind him to separate hero worship from respect born of necessity.

"Lin," he said warmly. "Haven't seen much of you lately."

Lin and Juarez both turned. "Oh, Alan," said the younger man. "It's good to see you."

Alan stopped before him and noted how Lindsay's frame filled out the flight uniform, how his shock of hair stood even with his own, the way his facial features had matured. "I can't get over it," he said, "the way you've grown up. I still remember you as the boy calling me Captain all the time."

Lindsay shrugged. "That was a long time ago. Things have a way of changing."

Alan thought back to the dining deck, and he looked down at Lindsay's polished boots beside Juarez's scuffed footwear. "Yes," he said quietly, "they do."

"Well, what brings you up here, *Captain*?" Juarez snickered at his own caustic words. He glanced at the crewmen. "Hear that, you scum? This skinny old man here used to be called *Captain*."

A couple of pirates looked over and grinned, but Alan's focus was squarely on Juarez, and he took a step toward him. "Don't push me," he warned angrily.

"Just what the hell you gonna do about it? Get that whore of yours to wear me out so bad I couldn't stand?"

Alan's fingers tensed as he glared at the pirate. "You leave her out of this. You hear me? Just leave her out of this! I'll kill anybody that touches her, and that includes you, *Captain Juarez*."

Juarez poked a finger in his chest. "You're the one better watch it. Or would you like to end up like that Thalian on the dining deck?"

"Come on, Alan, forget it," petitioned Lindsay, pulling him away. "We've got other things to worry about—Poteet."

Alan kept up his glare for long seconds, unbridled hatred seething in every part of his being. Then he breathed deeply and walked away a few steps.

"All this Poteet business of yours, Burke," said Juarez. "Here we've risked our necks getting to Myolia. How the hell you planning on finding one little ship in the middle of a solar system? Some captain you must've been."

Alan pivoted about. "If you're half the pirate you think you are, you wouldn't have to ask. Lindsay knows. He's worked this system with me before, back when he was a kid." He looked at the younger man. "I'm surprised you haven't explained it to him, Lin."

Lindsay cleared his throat and shifted uneasily. "I wasn't very old then."

Again Alan confronted Juarez. "There's only one reason the U.S.S. is in this system. They mine titanium on the second planet and ship it by freighter to the third planet to be refined. I worked this system for six months once. Poteet was with me. We figured out the shipping lanes, where the asteroid base was located. We knew where to lurk so we couldn't be found and knew when to attack.

"If he's still here, it's to prey on those freighters, and I know just where to look."

Juarez exhaled contemptuously. "That two-bit thief's not anywhere around here."

Alan stiffened and scowled at him. "What makes you so sure?"

Juarez motioned to the porthole. "Look at it! What would he be doing fooling around with freighters when he could have Faroul?"

Alan looked at him for long seconds before glancing at Lindsay. "You know," he said, nodding, "that's a good question." His eyes narrowed on the pirate. "Now why would anyone fool around with all this little stuff *for nine years* if he knew all the time how to get to the place that would make him a god?"

Juarez shifted nervously. "I'm the one asked *you* that." He slung a hand toward the crewmen. "I don't even know what's going on inside the head of my own scum here, so how you think I'd know anything about one of yours?"

The black man spun from his navigational post. "Juarez. Something's shown up on the sensors."

Juarez rushed to the station with Lindsay close behind. Leaning over the navigator's shoulder, the pirate studied the grid with multicolored blips flashing across.

"Hell!" Juarez exclaimed, beads of sweat popping out on his forehead. "It's fighters. A bunch of 'em!"

The black Thalian quickly pressed a series of buttons, each one singing out a musical tone, and gained a better reading. "There's ten, maybe eleven." He eyed the main controls at his fingertips. "Better tell me what to do. They're closing fast, speeding like everything."

Alan's arteries began to throb and he ran over to view the scanner blips for himself, memories deluging him. He had seen this before, dozens of times. He had stood on a control deck watching an attack formation and felt an iciness crawl down his back.

"They're starting to flank us," muttered the Thalian. "We better do something. Fast!"

Juarez's eye began twitching. He tried to summon a deep breath, but his lungs seemed as empty as the vacuum outside. "I . . ." He shook his head. "Reverse engines! We gotta outrun 'em!"

"No!" said Alan, and suddenly all eyes were on him.

"Get out of here!" ordered Juarez, shoving him in the chest.

Alan stumbled back and then righted himself. A part of him wanted to leap at the pirate, but abruptly, for the first time in nine years, he felt at home again.

"Look!" he told Juarez. "Their formation—it's like a reverse V— they're circling us! Those speedy little fighters will be bunched up behind us waiting to blow us to hell by the time we get this thing turned around!"

"He's right!" agreed the black man. "They're flanking us on a course that'll surround us!"

"Sub-light communication, Juarez!" blurted another crewman, adjusting receivers in his ears as he looked up at the pirate. "They demand our ship number and designated route." He squinted, placing a hand over his ear. "They say we've come too close to the shipping lanes, that they'll attack in thirty seconds if we don't acknowledge."

"Reverse engines, I told you!" yelled Juarez.

"That's just what they're expecting!" argued Alan. "They think we'll turn and run and they'll be there waiting for us." He leaned forward to the scanner screen, pressing his finger into the point of the V. "There! The rear! Dead ahead! There's only one fighter standing in our way. Full throttle! Attack it! Don't ever retreat. Attack and we'll blow the hell out of them!"

Juarez glanced at Alan. The pirate's hand quivered against his beard. "I . . ." He shook his head, slinging sweat from his brow.

"Ten seconds!" cried the crewman. He spun to Juarez. "Tell me what to do! Tell me or we're dead!"

Juarez shuddered and looked through the porthole at the points of light swiftly flanking them like speeding stars. But it was the single craft dead ahead that gleamed in his eyes.

"Full power!" he shouted. "Go straight for him!"

The black man gripped the controls with hands stiffened like bludgeons. A sudden jerk flung Alan backward, and Juarez and Lindsay careened with him to the scream of nuclear engines. Alan struck something immovable and sank, the G forces pinning him against metal as his larynx pushed against the back of his throat.

He clutched at a computer console, fought against many times his weight to pull himself up and stare at the single fighter growing in size like a supernova.

"More sub-light contact!" exclaimed the communications crewman. "They say turn back or they'll open fire!"

"The hell with them!" shouted Alan. "Fire the number one and two warheads. *Now*!"

A lever slammed downward. Fists depressed buttons. A missile streamed outward, then another, lighting up the blackness with red and blue flames like cannon fire in the night.

"Nuclear warhead on a direct course for us!" yelled the navigator.

Juarez suddenly was on his feet, his fingers seizing Alan by the collar. "I'll have you killed for this!" he screamed. "*I* give the orders! *I* tell when to fire!"

"Collision course, twelve seconds!" shouted the black man. "You bastard, tell me what to do!"

Juarez's hands remained at Alan's collar, and then he began to shake, his eyes wide and glazed.

Alan shoved him aside. "Out of my way!" He looked up and saw the incoming warhead like a blazing meteor at point-blank range. "Thirty-five degree tilt! Cut power!"

Fingers pushed buttons at the last instant. The ship swerved. The missile screamed by on the larboard side, mere seconds before their own warhead detonated against the fighter, spawning myriad colors so ineffably bright that Alan slung a forearm across his eyes.

"The fighters are turning, coming back for us!" reported the black man, watching the blips on the scanner.

Alan spun to Juarez, who still stood shuddering. "If you're giving orders around here, you sure as hell better tell him to hit full power back on our original course, or those fighters will be on us again!"

"I . . ." Juarez didn't seem to be able to find a breath. "Original course!" he managed, his voice a hoarse whisper. "Open throttle!"

A minute passed, then two, as the ship sped through the debris of the destroyed fighter. It lay strewn in open space, a million pieces of twisted metal and shattered glass, swirling like concentric waves fleeing from disturbed water.

The black man stared at the blips on the screen. Juarez turned to survey every pirate on deck. An ashen Lindsay gained his feet to look on wide-eyed. And Alan watched the universe race toward him at tremendous speed, yet the faraway constellations never seemed to grow nearer.

"We've lost 'em, Juarez," said the black man. "They've given up the chase. We've outdistanced 'em."

Alan turned to Juarez. "If you'd have consulted me about our course, let me know our coordinates in the system, this never would've happened. I'd've known when to cross the shipping lanes and when not to."

The pirate leader snorted. "If you hadn't been so busy with that whore of yours, you'd've known without me telling you."

"Let's don't bring her into this again, Juarez," pleaded Lindsay. He looked at Alan. "I told you from the start not to bring her. You knew how it would be."

"No," said Alan angrily, "I didn't know how a lot of things would turn out." He studied the computer readouts before turning to Juarez. "Set coordinates to zero point one-three-five in twenty-three seconds. If Poteet's around, that should take us right along his path."

He turned and started toward the hatch.

"Better get back to her," said Juarez caustically. "You know, I get the feeling she does a man *good*, now doesn't she?"

Alan stopped and faced the bearded man, whose fingers still trembled. "You think you could handle a woman?" He smiled and shook his head. "You can't even handle a starship."

Before Juarez could protest, Alan squeezed through the hatch.

He met Davon on a lower level in a corridor near their quarters. She wore a worried expression.

"Alan! The ship, the engines. What's the matter?"

He stopped before her, looking at the smooth skin, the uniform with the top two buttons undone.

"Trouble, U.S.S. fighter craft. We made it. This time."

"Something's wrong," she said quietly. "With you and Juarez."

He frowned and took her hands. "I don't know what to make of you sometimes. There's times I seem to know you, and then there's times . . ."

She shrugged. "There's trouble here. I'm not sure what's going to happen, but . . ." Abruptly her face paled.

"What is it, Davon? What is it you see?"

She stared at him, and then looked away. "You're a man of inter-stellar travel, one that's heard all that science has to say since you first joined the U.S.S." She turned back to him. "How can I expect you to believe all the things I've told you?"

"Who said I didn't?"

"No," she said sharply. "You listen and nod your head, but you don't believe I see things that will happen, just like you laughed at me when I told you about my mother."

"Oh, Davon," he said impatiently, "I didn't laugh at you. I just think there's a lot of things that are natural occurrences. When somebody doesn't understand them, they automatically attribute it to a deity or something."

She gripped his arm. "Look at me, Alan Burke. Look into my eyes and tell me there's nothing but scientific laws at work in the universe. Tell me we're all here by freak accident, that there's no meaning to any of us living."

He exhaled strongly. "I have a reason. Destroy anybody that does me wrong."

She frowned. "You say you can't understand me, but what about you? There's such bitterness and hatred. But at other times you can be so gentle and caring."

"I care about anybody that treats me fair."

She glanced down as if pondering his words. "There's something else in my life, Alan, something I've never told anyone. When I was little, lying in bed one night, there was a light, a beam so bright I couldn't see anything else, yet I wasn't scared of it. It was like it spoke to me, told me things would happen in my life like they were meant to. I reached out for it and it seemed to fill me with warmth, make me feel strong, cared for. Ever since then, I've known things, seen things I shouldn't."

Alan drew back, a sudden cold encompassing him like clouds rolling in over a mountain. He put a hand to his head, remembering that last time in his cell, how he had reached out for the light, felt it warm and strengthen him—and how he had stood before the porthole and sensed the same sensation.

"Alan? What's wrong? What did I—"

He inhaled deeply. "I . . . I'm tired. I'm going to my cabin, sleep."

Chapter Twelve

For several days, the ship scouted the area parallel to the shipping lanes, ranging from Myolia I where the titanium was mined, past the orbit of the asteroid star base, and on toward the refineries on Myolia III.

The sensors detected space debris, meteoroid swarms, a small comet, and scattered asteroids up to a kilometer in diameter. But there was no sign of Poteet's ship, not even in areas where Alan and he once had lurked prior to attacks on freighters.

As the days lingered, Davon felt increasingly uneasy, as though a dark cloud shrouded the ship. Sometimes the sense of gloom was deeply personal, and she would break into a cold sweat or grow faint, even in the supposed security of her cabin.

Juarez! He had done it once, and she knew with dry mouth and weak knees that it was only a matter of time before . . .

No. She wouldn't think about it. She would put it out of her mind, dwell upon the sudden sense of purpose she had found in Alan.

She stood bathing in the Catholian Ray one evening, feeling her naked skin tingle as it was cleansed, warmed. Her hair cascaded across her breasts and she looked down at her sleek legs.

A body.

That's all she had ever been to anyone, ever since she had retreated to the bordellos of Thalia, where she had gained escape from starvation at the price of her dignity. She ran her fingers lightly along her arm and began to quake. No one had ever understood or cared. From the time she had been four, everyone had stood apart from her, chanting or running with fear. The only life she had ever really known had been the seductive smile and nod that had summoned hundreds of drunkards, thieves, sadomasochists.

And all for her body.

Until now.

Alan. A beaten man with a battered body, but one whose spirit had never broken. He had been defeated by time, by the mines, but not yet destroyed.

He was different from the rest. Somehow when he looked at her, held her in his arms, he seemed to see her as more than a desirable body. Yet she was confused about her feelings toward him. They seemed to transcend the physical, though in every touch of his hand, every tender kiss, there was desire on her part.

He could have taken her anytime he wanted, but he hadn't. And waves of happiness swept through her, for she knew that unlike the patrons in the house of delights, he cared about her.

He cared!

Alan! she cried to herself, remembering the years of loneliness, rejection, the lusting men who had used her like a lemstel keg to be discarded. She loved him! She loved him and wanted to share life with him!

Davon hated to leave her quarters during those long days as the craft sped parallel to the freighter route. She hated sitting in the dining area, feeling Juarez's eyes on her, seeing his smug smile and realizing that he was remembering and anticipating. She grew jittery every time the intercom announced that the artificial food was prepared. She wanted only to lie on her jet mattress and shut the world out of her mind.

But she couldn't, for Alan made a point of escorting her to every meal.

She couldn't lose him. Not the one person in all the galaxy who made her feel like a woman again, who gave her a reason to grit her teeth and struggle on. She couldn't let him die all because she had once been a prostitute.

Oh, Jesus, help me forget Juarez, to live with it! Don't let me weaken and tell Alan!

So she went to meals and saw the thin lips and yellowed teeth, heard again her own screams as his fingers had clawed at her.

No. She would not let herself think about it, even when she saw Juarez or brushed past him in the corridor.

For Alan, and he alone, she would bear it all herself.

***

It was four days by chronometer after the starship battle when Alan met Juarez on the stairwell between levels.

"Myolia III," said Juarez. "We've come millions of kilometers from Myolia I, and now we're almost to the refineries. And where's Poteet? You seemed so sure of yourself back there. Now what do you think of it all?"

Alan gripped the silvery rail and looked at the pirate framed by the stairwell's supporting posts. "Last definite word was that Poteet was working this system. You said so yourself first time we met. If he's not working the lanes, then he could be down dealing with the black market on Myolia III. We had contacts there nine, ten years ago. He might still be dealing with them. Anyway, they might know if he's still in the system or where he's headed."

"You know what I think?" snapped Juarez. "You've led us on a wild goose chase clear across interstellar space 'cause all you care about's getting Poteet, not Faroul. I'm not playing this game a minute more."

"You don't know him very well, do you? We were on the same ship together, five, six years. He's a bloodthirsty pirate who'd betray his own mother for half a dozen credits, but I've got to admit he's a brilliant tactician. You get in a fight with him, a starship fight, and he's got the know-how and guts to blow you to kingdom come and not blink an eye."

Alan nodded upward. "If he's out there, on his way to Faroul, and we show up, neither of the ships will come out unscathed. He can either surprise us or we can surprise him. It all depends on solid intelligence."

Juarez exhaled angrily. "What if he's not going at all? What if all these wild stories about him knowing the way are a bunch of lies? I don't care about him. I want Faroul!"

Alan studied the twitching beard. "Then you'd better slit my throat right now, because you'll never have it."

Juarez stepped toward him, eyes blazing. "You bastard, you're taking me there!"

Alan stood looking at him and just laughed. "I'll take you there, all right, but you'll never have Faroul. Nobody can ever have it except . . ."

Memories flooded him, and the words died away.

"Who?" cried Juarez. "Who can have it?"

Alan's chest rose. "Only power can," he whispered. "Nothing else in all the universe."

Juarez looked away with a wag of his head. "You're just a senile old man, you—"

"Myolia III," interrupted Alan. "I want the planetary module, two men to back me up. Go into orbit, let me go down, check the black market. You do that and I'll take you to Faroul, and you can have all of it you can keep."

Alan went into the crew's sleeping quarters and found Lindsay lying on a jet mattress on the lower level of a double bunk. Sweat permeated the air like the inside of a locker room, thanks to the body odor of a pirate asleep nearby with arm slung across face.

"Lin," said Alan, stopping before the young man with closed eyes. "I want to talk to you."

Lindsay looked up and stretched lazily. "Oh, Alan." He yawned. "Guess you caught me snoozing." He sat up, slinging his legs over the edge.

"I'm going down to Myolia III, check on Poteet in the black market."

Lindsay's eyes widened. "I'll go with you."

Alan shook his head. "Just me and a couple of crewmen. That's all the module will hold. I want you to stay here. Do something for me, for old time's sake."

Lindsay frowned.

"It's Davon," Alan said. "I know you don't like her—"

"I never said that."

"Yeah, but from the start you didn't want her along."

"I was right. You see all the trouble she's caused?"

Alan felt blood fill his cheeks. "Now listen, Lin, I didn't come in here to argue with you. I came to ask you to look out for her, take care of her in case I . . . ." He shook his head and ran his fingers along the edge of the upper bunk. "You know how it is in the black market."

Lindsay stood. "Sure, Alan, if that's what you want. But I'd still like to come along. You might need me."

"I need you here more."

Lindsay looked directly into his face. "You really think that much of her, don't you? A prostitute out of the slums and you think that much of her. Deep inside, you know I'm right about her not belonging here, not when we're going to Faroul."

"I'm worried about you too, Lin, the way you've changed."

"I haven't changed, I've just grown up. I'm not the little boy hanging on to your pants leg anymore."

"That's part of it, maybe," acknowledged Alan. "But there's other things I see in you I wish I didn't. I see greed and way too much ambition ruling your every thought and action."

Lindsay's expression grew defensive. "Just like revenge rules you?"

Alan sighed deeply. "I always thought the world of you, Lin. There wasn't anything I wouldn't have done for you. You were a scared little boy that needed somebody. But if truth be told, I needed you every bit as bad as you did me.

"I'd seen my father killed, turned my back on the U.S.S., got mixed up with scum that didn't care if I lived or died, and then you came along. You looked up to me, made me feel needed, gave me something to live for besides vengeance and bitterness.

"I know what's ruled me, Lin. You don't have to tell me. But what would you have done? If you'd seen your father killed by the U.S.S.?"

Lindsay swallowed hard and stared into his eyes. "You forget, Alan," he said hoarsely. "I did."

Alan dropped his gaze, feeling his own words pierce him. He looked up, started to speak, but hesitated until he could formulate his thoughts. "I . . . I'm sorry, Lin. Sorry I didn't think, made you remember."

As he turned to the corridor, his thoughts raged like a maelstrom.

Chapter Thirteen

The planetary module separated from the mother ship and was alone in space, a tiny silver bird framed against the blue oceans and grayish-brown continents below, where wispy white clouds rolled like breakers in a sea.

Alan set a computer course for Ruijen, the great interstellar shipping port and refinery center, and leaned back and remembered.

He recalled the years as pirate captain, when he had learned to attack what he feared, and do it with savagery. But those challenges had been different. They had consisted of outside forces. Now he had to deal with himself.

He thought about Davon, listened again as she told him of his bitterness. He remembered denouncing Lin for the factors that motivated him, only to realize that something just as destructive ruled his own life.

But what did they know? They didn't share the unique experiential background that had shaped his outlook. No one knew what was really inside him, the confusing blend of concern and vindictiveness that had given him a reason for living ever since he first had held a dead falcon.

The sun became a fiery torch ahead as the craft swung onward across the world toward the dawn, and there was light.

Light!

There was something else inside him now, something that had given him purpose ever since that last time in the cell. But he couldn't quite grasp it, for it seemed distant, hazy, separated from him by thick fog, a battlement of fire.

An hour later Alan and two pirates walked the noonday streets in the slums of Ruijen and looked at the people who crowded the walkways: hollow-eyed drunkards and lemstel addicts sprawling in trash beneath stairwells . . . merchants bartering black market linens and jewelry . . . women with cracked faces standing before bars and brothels . . . young boys, suitcases of wares in arm, pleading with passersby to purchase goods.

He saw them all—the young who would become the old, and the old who would become the lost—and he saw himself, a deserter running away from all that he had found life to be. He had lost himself in places such as this, in the smell of sweat and vomit and the feel of lemstel dribbling down his chin.

What had it gotten him?

Nothing more than a pirate crew, betrayal, and something worse than the loss of nine years.

Was it his own dignity that had been the greatest casualty? Had he sacrificed honor for vengeance? What was the matter with him? Why couldn't he concentrate anymore, clear his cluttered thoughts?

A few minutes later Alan and the two pirates sat at a wobbly table in a dimly lighted back room that smelled of sweat and leche weed. With a creak, the door opened and the threshold framed a medium-sized man with a pot belly and a ring of gray hair. His eyes were mere slits as he surveyed the three men and focused on Alan.

"You," he said, closing the door behind him and coming nearer. "I can't quite . . . don't remember your name."

Alan stood, his chair scraping the scarred floor, and extended his hand across the table. "Burke. Used to deal titanium with you ten, eleven years back."

The man ignored Alan's hand and pulled out a chair. "I thought you were dead," he commented, sitting down. He took out a bag of leche weed and roll of paper. "Care for any?"

Alan eased into his chair. One leg was shorter than the rest. "No, thanks."

One of the pirates reached for the bag. "I'll take some."

The pot-bellied man looked straight at Alan. He nodded toward the pair. "Better tell your men I deal only with the top dog, not dirty little thieves."

Alan looked at the two pirates, whose countenances showed anger. "Just let me handle it." He turned back to the man, who lighted a leche cigarette and took a deep drag. "Poteet. I'm looking for him."

The black market trader exhaled smoke through his nose to let it spiral upward. "You and every U.S.S. patrol from here to Buquerque."

"I heard he was working this system."

The man shrugged and scratched his chin. "Yeah," he snarled. "He made a deal to bring me a big load from Myolia I several months back. Then he up and disappeared on me."

Alan leaned forward with elbows on table. "Where'd he go?"

"How should I know? Dealing with him's like dealing with a snake. You never know what he's going to do next. Last I heard, there was some crazy talk about him trying to find Faroul."

"Is that what he set out for?"

"I'm *through* dealing with him. I don't care where he goes, the swine. He was always talking about Faroul, saying he was going to work out some kind of plan to get there."

"What's that mean?"

The man stood. "I thought you came here to do business, not ask a bunch of silly questions. I ain't no tourist guide. If that's all you want, just get the hell out of my place."

Alan's chest expanded, and he looked at his companions. "Let's go."

They stood and started toward the door as the black marketer scowled at them. When Alan came abreast of the man, he stopped and glared. "You know something?" he snapped. "I always did think you were a pig. Now I *know* it."

They left.

***

Alan had been away several hours when Juarez brushed past Lindsay in the corridor outside the commissary.

"Hey," said Lindsay, reaching for his arm.

Juarez spun, his face filling with blood. He looked down at the fingers closed on his sleeve, digits against dingy nylon.

Lindsay looked too, and his fingers grew limp. He muffled a cough. "I heard you sent Alan down to Ruijen to check on Poteet."

Juarez rubbed his nose into his shoulder. "You heard right."

"But—"

"But what? Now listen, you little wimp. I've gone ahead and played Burke's silly game, but I'm sick and tired of it. We made a deal to get to Faroul, and all he does is run around playing chase with somebody that's not even there. I've put up with all I'm going to."

Lindsay lowered his head. "You don't understand Burke. He doesn't care about Faroul. I'm beginning to wonder if he ever believed in it. He had a chance to go, back before Poteet got him sent up, but he didn't."

Juarez stepped nearer, until he was right in Lindsay's face. "Then just how am I supposed to get to Faroul? What *does* he care about?"

"All he wants is Poteet. If he thinks Poteet's out there he'll do everything in his power to go after him."

And if he decides he's *not* out there?"

Lindsay shrugged. "He wouldn't even tell *me* how to get to Faroul. I thought he would, but he wouldn't."

Juarez wagged his head in disgust, and for long moments there was only the clatter of silverware against platter from the dining deck. "That friend of yours, he's nobody's fool. I could see that from the start. I let him drag us all the way to Myolia just because he didn't buy the rumor that Poteet's headed for Faroul."

"But you let him go down to the black market. What if he finds out something, finds out Poteet's not going?"

"What's there for him to find out?" Juarez retorted. "I thought nobody knew *where* Poteet's at." He poked a finger in Lindsay's chest. "You get this straight. Deal was, I get part of Faroul. If I don't . . ." He didn't finish. "I just hope he don't see you for the spineless little weasel you really are. Now get out of my way. I'm paying a visit to that pretty whore of his."

The pirate turned and started down the corridor. Lindsay stood watching his boot heels rise and fall, feeling the vibration every time they clicked against metal. He wanted to say something, to tell him no, to come back, leave her alone.

"Juarez, I don't think . . ."

The pirate wheeled, his beard twitching. He stood framed in the corridor, a menacing silhouette against the lights along the walls. "You don't think *what*?"

Lindsay stammered, the words lodging in his throat. He hung his head and slunk away toward the dining deck.

And with every step, the pirate's sinister laugh pierced his skin like barbs on a prison fence.

***

Davon spent the shift waiting for Alan to escort her to the late meal. Resting in her quarters behind a locked door, she stared at the overhead light and tried to delineate what she saw, as an artist might seek to decipher a smeared painting. Sometimes the mist cleared like a fog broken by sudden breeze and she thought she could see herself, Alan, and a dark, sinister figure before them. And beyond rose a wall that eddied and blazed like fire that did not consume.

There was danger, death, destiny. She strained to see clearly until her eyes burned, her skull ached. But the images blurred and then faded, and she did not know the outcome.

She went to the elliptical porthole, a patch of darkness spangled with multi-colored stars like sequins on a black curtain. She could feel the coolness, see the reflection of her cheeks, hair, eyes. Just herself. Alone. Out of touch with others, with what everyone else considered life to be. And beyond lay only the mysterious reaches of space.

She could not help but wonder if the enigmas outside the porthole were as great as those inside her.

The emptiness consumed her, stirring memories of a thousand gloomy nights in which she had stood before a brothel window, her arms outstretched for someone, like Michelangelo's Adam reaching out with his hand for his Creator.

Something suddenly dented the barrier that surrounded her senses. She became alert, turning to the well-lighted quarters and waiting until she heard it again.

Her loneliness vanished like a log carried to sea by tide and she smiled. It was the rap of Alan's knuckles on the door.

She rushed across the cabin, longing for his comfort. She reached for the orange control button beside the jamb, but then started, as if someone had pricked her with a needle.

Something wasn't right. Strange intuition told her as much, or did it?

She put her cheek against the door. "Alan?"

There was no answer but the beating of her heart.

"Is that you, Alan?"

Now, Juarez's gruff voice answered. "Sorry filth had an accident on the shuttle. Better get out here. Quick."

Alan!

Still, her fingers hovered above the button.

"Stay there then," snarled Juarez. "I don't give a damn if he's asking for you."

She slapped her hand against the button and the door slid back. "What happened?" she exclaimed, looking into his blood-streaked eyes and beyond his shoulder. "Where is he? Tell me what's wrong!"

Juarez's tangled beard parted in a sneer. "Ain't *nothin'* wrong now," he growled.

She realized too late and couldn't elude his sudden grip. She cried out and tried to pull away, but the pirate only laughed cruelly and dragged her across the cabin. She could feel his putrid breath in her face, smell the sickening odor of sweat and lemstel.

"I like a woman like you," he said, his mouth drooling as she flailed at him, "like 'em with a little fight."

She broke through his guard and caught him hard in mouth, but it served only to anger him. He winced and cursed, and then inspected a trickle of blood that disappeared in his beard.

"Ain't no cheap whore hits *me*," he said, backhanding her in the mouth.

She sank to the floor, much as she had that last night in the palace of delights. Gaining her knees, she clawed at the floor in an attempt to escape, but the pirate was like a cat toying with a mouse. He let her manage a couple of meters and then seized her ankle, only to allow her to kick free again. Finally he tired of the game and clutched her with a vise-like grip.

Looking up, Davon found him licking the blood on his mouth as he laughed quietly.

****

Poteet.

He remained in Alan's mind like a throbbing tumor all the way into orbit. He strained to recreate the scene from memory: Kasterfayette sprawled limply on a jet mattress, his face like chalk and his lips tremulous . . . the overhead fluorescent light reflecting from his gray eyes and balding head with stringy white hair . . . Poteet at Alan's elbow, leaning close to make out the words like wind whispering through a forest.

Alan had turned, nodded to the door. "Go on outside."

Poteet had stiffened, his chest filling with air. "What?"

"The door," Alan had said. "Leave me alone with him."

Alan remembered how Poteet's eyes had become like a knife edge flickering in sunlight, how he had looked down at Kasterfayette's cracked lips and then surveyed Alan coldly.

"Now!" Alan had ordered.

Poteet's temples had flushed like an aging red sun. He had stammered and cursed under his breath before turning and walking for the door.

Yes, thought Alan, it had happened that way. Poteet had left and only one person had heard the full details of Kasterfayette's story.

But the room-to-room intercom. No, he told himself, the switch near the porthole above the bed had remained untouched.

He frowned, his memory reeling, eyes aching from deep inside. What about the second control near the doorway? He rubbed the back of his neck and felt his joints stiffen. Had he watched Poteet until the door had slid shut, separating him from Kasterfayette's dying breaths? He relived the moment again and again, remembering how Poteet's heels had slammed into the floor, the way his fists had swung at his side.

Why couldn't he remember seeing the door open, close? Had he turned to feel the old man's fingers seize his arm before Poteet had reached the control panel?

Why was he so uncertain whether the image of a door whishing open, then shut, was true memory or just the result of dwelling on the matter so long?

He clenched his hand. A seemingly insignificant detail nine and a half years ago, and now his head swam because of it!

The computer-controlled module rendezvoused with the spacecraft a thousand kilometers above the white-streaked seas splotched with land masses like mud slung on a portrait. Minutes after docking Alan was ascending the stairways that led to the upper levels, and with each impact of boot against grill he tried to decide what he should do.

Poteet! He longed to sink his fingers into his larynx, choke him until his eyes became unseeing and his face whitened like sunlight against fog.

Poteet had betrayed him! He had betrayed him and he must pay! If he had to search the entire galaxy for the rest of his life, he would find Poteet and kill him!

Alan reached the level where the cabins lay and grasped a rail to ascend higher. Then he glimpsed Lindsay walking down the corridor, his boot heels clicking.

"Lin!" He released the banister and stepped onto the floor.

Lindsay spun to become framed in the corridor ten meters distant. "Alan. I-I didn't expect you back this soon." His eyes shifted nervously, as if avoiding eye contact.

Alan approached as the overhead lights reflected in his boots. "Didn't take long, not to find out all I did."

Lindsay straightened, but he continued to avoid Alan's gaze. "What did they say?" His voice was as quiet as the flow of air from the vents.

Alan shook his head and stopped before him. "Guess when you've been dead nine years, everybody forgets how much you did for them. The guy I used to run titanium for, he treated me like a dog, ordered me out."

Lindsay pressed nervous fingers against belt buckle. "Poteet," he said quietly.

Alan exhaled sharply and bit his lip. "Not here, at least not anymore. Talk is he's trying to get to Faroul, all right."

Now, Lindsay found his eyes. "That's what I've been trying to tell you."

"Yeah." He gritted his teeth. "I just want to live long enough to catch up with him. Juarez. Where's he at?"

Lindsay shifted uneasily and muffled a cough. "I . . . Upstairs, in the control room."

Alan acknowledged with a nod, and then glanced over the younger man's shoulder. "Seen Davon?"

I . . . uh . . ." Lindsay shuddered and cleared his throat. "Not since first meal."

"Think I'll look in on her," he said, starting for the third door on the left.

Lindsay whirled after him. "Alan, I . . ."

Alan hesitated. "What's wrong, Lin? You look white as a sheet."

"I . . . I don't think she's there."

Alan took a step toward him, concerned as he tried to read the younger man's expression. "You said you hadn't seen her."

Lindsay glanced at the floor and shrugged. "I'd forgotten. The dining deck, I-I think I saw her, saw her . . . sitting there eating a while ago."

"No," Alan said with authority. "She hasn't left her cabin without me in days."

He pivoted and continued to the door.

"I *know* I saw her, Alan," Lindsay contended from behind. "She asked about you. I-I told her you'd be gone several hours."

A hand abruptly was on Alan's upper arm, and he turned to see Lindsay's face contorted with fright, the eyes wide and wild. *"For God's sake, Alan, don't go in there!"*

Alan swallowed hard and pulled free. He slapped the heel of his hand against the button. The door hummed and slid open, and the details of the cabin flooded his mind like successive shock waves. Bare skin. A man, woman. Arms, legs entangled on the floor beneath the porthole. Hair in disarray. Clothes strewn wildly. Groans and breaths as heavy as an animal's.

The moment seemed frozen in time. He withdrew a step, as if vicious winds slammed into his chest. A violent shudder gripped him, his collapsing lungs screaming for air. A cry he could not utter was on his lips, and then a guttural rose up from deep in his throat.

"Bastard! Filthy bastard!"

He rushed across the cabin, his entire being fixed on the bearded man who whirled with neck veins bulging like overflowing rivers.

"What the hell!" exclaimed Juarez.

The pirate rolled to his hip and threw up an arm to ward off the attack. Davon, suddenly free, turned to slash at the floor with her fingernails.

Alan slapped Juarez's arm away and drove a savage knee into his ribs as he fell upon him. The pirate groaned and collapsed. Alan's fist glanced off his jaw, but spirit and the element of surprise could carry an Alosian mines survivor only so far. With superior strength, the pirate grasped his hair, wrenched his head back, and slung him aside with a gouging elbow to the mouth.

The overhead lights flashed in Alan's eyes, and then a silhouetted fist fell toward him. He rolled, absorbing the blow on his cheekbone.

"I'll kill you!" Juarez shrieked, his knuckles trickling with blood.

He climbed off the floor to gain leverage for a vicious kick, but Alan doubled him over with a heel to the groin. Now, both men were hurt, and when Alan managed to struggle up, they faced off like two dazed rams.

"Afraid that whore's not chargin' enough?" grunted Juarez, grimacing and still unable to stand erect.

Alan glanced at Davon, who sat against the wall, clutching clothes to her breast.

The pirate waved him in. "Come on! What you waitin' for?" Blood ran down the corner of his mouth. "Maybe she charged me too much!"

"You're lying!"

Juarez forced a snicker through the pain. "Am I?" He twirled a thumb at the woman. "Why don't you ask her?"

Alan swung a roundhouse left that grazed the pirate's beard, but then took a counterpunch to the temple.

"Go on, ask her!"

Two lefts and a right caught Alan in the forehead, neck. He staggered, blocked an amateurish uppercut with his arm, and saw a fist in his eyes. Then the lights turned fuzzy and the floor came up to collide with his shoulder.

"Stop it!" screamed Davon, crawling toward them. "Stop it!"

Alan was back on Alos. He shook his head, trying to brush away the mine dust. A handbeam was a brilliant mass of fire before his eyes, and the sinister figure of a guard loomed behind it.

"Tell him!" snapped Juarez, glaring at Davon and then kicking Alan in the face. "Tell him or I'll kill the dog!"

"Yes!" she cried. The yell echoed through the cabin, piercing Alan's fog, a blow worse than anything Juarez could deliver. "I let him, let him do anything he wanted! Just stop it!"

There was a commotion at the doorway. Hazy beyond Juarez, three crewmen with drawn Bannings entered while Lindsay stood and watched. Juarez turned to them.

"Drag him up," he ordered.

Alan shook his head, trying to distinguish the dancing images. Rough hands slid under his arms from behind, jerking, lifting, supporting. They twisted his arms behind his back, and he was helpless to do anything but wince.

Full awareness struck him with the touch of a Banning muzzle above his ear.

"Kill him?" asked the man behind the weapon.

"No!" yelled Lindsay, and all eyes turned to the flushed young man who came nearer. "You lose him and you lose Faroul!"

"The hell with Faroul!" exclaimed Juarez. "He ain't taking us nowhere! He never has been!"

Lindsay nodded to Alan. "He knows the way, only him! You kill him and we'll never get to Faroul, never have the power to create. None of us!"

"I'm tired of all his stalling!" Juarez snarled. He grabbed Alan by the collar, drawing him viciously to his face. "You tell me now or I'll kill you! You hear me? I'll kill you!"

A guard twisted Alan's arm. The Banning muzzle jabbed into his skull. He could see the broken blood vessels like tiny rivers of fire in Juarez's eyes and smell the lemstel on his breath.

Davon suddenly was on her feet, her face deluged with emotion. "Tell him!" she cried to Alan. "Tell him, damn you!"

Alan spun, jerking free of the pirate's hands, and looked at Davon with penetrating eyes. She stood two meters away, lips quaking, hair strewn like confetti. He studied her smudged cheeks, naked shoulders, the flight uniform she drew across her curves, green material against white skin.

But it was her eyes that captivated him, as they had light years away in a palace of delights when he first had seen her. He stared into them, seeing a reflection of himself, an escapee from Alos, lost, alone, searching. And then he saw himself regaining dreams, hopes, desires, not because he was free and in pursuit of Poteet, but because of the tender touch, soft voice, and caring he had found in a woman whom fate had cast into his life.

Her words still strafed his mind, absorbed into every cell, his very soul reeling from them. *"I let him, let him do anything he wanted!"*

In her, he had found something that had been missing from his life from his first moment of awareness. And now, that very hope had shattered like a porthole yielding to the mysterious loneliness of the universe.

He didn't care anymore. Not about Poteet. Or freedom. Or Faroul.

He had put his trust in someone again, only to be betrayed.

"I'm sorry, Davon," he whispered, "sorry I thought you were more."

Lindsay came up with a note pad and pen and shoved them into his hands. "The coordinates. Write down the coordinates."

Alan's eyes never left Davon's. She stood there shaking, the clothes across her torso rippling in the air vent breeze.

Silence. An eon of quietness. Thoughts. Disintegration.

He took the pen, felt its roundness. The paper fluttered and rustled in his palm. Without looking down he scribbled a set of numbers. His fingers became loose and the pen dropped to the floor.

Juarez snatched the paper from his hand and read it hurriedly. He squinted, and then nodded and motioned to the guards. "Take him to the freight bay, chain him up."

The two guards began escorting Alan away and he did not resist. As they neared the door he looked back at Davon, noting her tangled hair across her face, the reflection of the lights in her moist eyes.

Her lips trembled. "Alan, I . . ."

Her voice became a sob, and she turned and buried her face in her hands as they whisked him away.

Chapter Fourteen

Davon stood looking through the porthole at a blurred galaxy as she slipped on her flight shirt and fastened the buttons.

"Your men," she heard Lindsay tell Juarez. "Did you see the way they looked at her?" There was a long moment filled only with Davon's quiet sobs. "It's been a long time since port. Why don't you let them have her?"

She turned, defiance in her eyes. She glared at Lindsay, and when he saw her he seemed to shrink back.

"Alan—I thought you were his friend!" she said angrily. "I thought you cared about him, then you just stand there and let him get beaten! Now me, *this*. From the start I knew you hated me, wanted to get rid of me. Tell me why!"

Lindsay glanced at Juarez, who stood staring at him. The bearded pirate nodded to Davon. "Why don't you tell her?"

The younger man faced her. "I hated you because of what you've done to Alan. You've made him stop thinking about Faroul, even about Poteet. You've caused everybody to be at each other's throats. I want Faroul, you whore, and all you've done is jeopardize everything."

Davon's breast expanded and she took a step toward him. "No. You hate me because there's something inside of you that makes you afraid of me. You haven't even processed it yourself, but you're scared."

Juarez laughed. "That little wimp's afraid of his own shadow." He looked at Lindsay. "Now get out before I give you something to be scared of!"

Lindsay opened his mouth to respond, but lowered his head and slunk away.

Davon watched until the door hummed shut behind him, and then looked Juarez and found him smiling smugly. "You think nobody can touch you," she said, "that you're king of this ship, that everybody licks your boots. But I promise you, next time you come in here, you're going to die."

Juarez leaned his head back and laughed. He reached for his shirt and began putting it on. "And just who's gonna do it? That skinny old man I beat hell out of?"

Something cold and calculating took hold of Davon. "No. I am."

Juarez grinned, the yellow lemstel stains on his teeth showing. "Well, we'll just see about that, now won't we? How about next shift? Or maybe you'd like my whole crew instead?"

Snickering, he walked out the door.

***

Alan sat in the shadows of the freight bay and felt the manacles bite into his wrists. They hurt, but something else hurt more.

He brought his hands to his forehead. The chains rattled and screeched as they swung inside the freight hook on the wall above. He rubbed his eyes and felt his breath in spurts against his palms. When he stretched out his legs and lay back, he found his bonds so short that his hands dangled at chain's length above his head.

He was tired. His muscles ached. He was hungry and his mouth was dry. His mind seemed clouded, uncertain, but he was still aware enough to understand that he suffered mental, physical, and emotional exhaustion, to the point of not caring anymore.

No, that was not like him. Even when things had seemed their darkest in the dungeons, even when the rats had gnawed at his skin, he still had clung to hatred and Kasterfayette's words to stay alive. Now he couldn't muster even that. It was as if his entire being had assumed a passive existence, neither in charge of his fate nor wanting to be.

He tried to make a fist, but he seemed drained of energy and desire, like a desert cactus wrung of all moisture. Deep inside he could remember the emotions that had driven him, but they wouldn't surface, as if they had been crushed.

What now?

He shook his head. Did it matter anymore? Was there any reason to keep hanging on?

The United Star Systems. Poteet. Faroul. They seemed beyond his realm of existence, dim and unimportant.

And Davon.

He swallowed hard, feeling bumps rise along his arms. Why should he feel such bitterness toward her? Why should he feel so personally struck down? Whatever made him think that she owed him something, that some sort of bond existed between them?

Unless . . .

He shook himself, feeling his pulse throb. Chains clattered and he clutched at the hook in the wall.

Davon!

He wanted her, this escapee from the Thalian brothels. Not the U.S.S. or Poteet or the power of creation, only her.

No. She had betrayed him, laughed at him behind his back, told him how much she feared Juarez and then . . .

Now he managed a fist. She had betrayed him, and he could never forget it.

***

During the sleep period Davon slipped quietly out of her cabin and hurried down the corridor. Descending to the lowest level, she started toward the freight bay.

Her eyes burned. Emotion choked her throat. The back of her head ached. And with each quick step, her legs quivered.

She had to see him, had to tell him the truth. She was angry at herself, at the world, because she had let him think the worst of her. Where had it gotten him, or her?

Alan! she thought, remembering his bitter denouncement of her. If he only knew what she had done for him, all for him. If he only realized how she had sacrificed her new-found dignity just to keep him from being hurt, killed.

And Juarez, he was coming back for her, again and again. And when he did, she would kill him or die.

When she neared the entrance to the freight bay she glimpsed the guard in the shadows and her breaths came faster. She slowed, trying to keep her sentiments from vanquishing her. Straightening her hair and smoothing her uniform, she approached.

The pirate, a tall brawny man with one ear severed at the lobe, sat leaning against the door jamb, puffing on a leche weed cigarette. She watched the red glow as he took a drag and tapped the ashes against his boot.

He looked up. "What are you doing here?" he challenged, rising.

She stopped before him, watching his eyes survey her up and down. "I want to see him."

"What for? Looks to me like you think you've found something better. Juarez, that pig, he thinks he owns us, owns this ship. Now a woman comes along and he thinks she's his too, that nobody else can touch her."

"He doesn't own me."

The pirate threw his cigarette butt to the floor and stomped it. "The pig thinks he can get away with anything."

Davon edged nearer, sensing an opportunity. "Then why do you let him? There's ten or eleven of you. You don't have to put up with him stealing from you."

"Yeah," snarled the pirate, "and *then* just what are we supposed to do? He's a filthy dog, but nobody else can captain this ship. Nobody else knows nothing, except . . ." He glanced strangely into the freight bay. "I heard Burke did pretty good the other day when all those fighters were on our butts. But he's just a sick old man, not even one of us."

"Can I see him a minute?"

The pirate again glanced inside the bay. "I don't know. Juarez said nobody's to go in."

"Are you that scared of him? Are all of you so scared of Juarez you won't do anything he says not to? I thought you were pirates, out here attacking U.S.S. ships, with courage enough to do anything if you had something to gain by it."

The pirate's eyes roamed her body again. He smiled, and Davon didn't like what she saw in his shadowy face.

"*I* got something to gain by letting you in?" he asked, eyebrows raised.

"The next man touches me, I'll kill him."

The pirate laughed and withdrew a pouch of leche weed to roll another cigarette. "I like you. At least you've got a little nerve, not scared of your own shadow."

He rolled the joint and lighted it, the flame from his lighter illuminating his bristly stubble. He took a deep drag and eased back down to the floor. He nodded to the entrance. "Go ahead."

Davon brushed past and entered the freight bay, where crates and boxes rose like monoliths in the shadows. She shivered, remembering the last time she had been here, and her steps became like echoes in catacombs.

Something stirred the night beneath the starry porthole. Metal grated against metal. A silhouette began to take shape on the floor.

She stopped, her nostrils singed by the nauseating odor of sweat and urine, and questioned her presence here. What could she say that would make any difference? Couldn't she already hear his contemptuous response?

"I . . ." It was all she could manage.

Alan took his upper arm from his brow. He was quiet for long seconds, as if studying and considering her. Then he flinched and turned away, leaving her to stare at the chain links that seemed so cold and gray against the black.

"It's you," he rasped.

She went nearer. "I . . . I have to talk to you, tell you some things."

He wouldn't look at her. "Go away."

"I can't," she half-sobbed. She ran her fingers along the crate at her shoulder. "It's you that got me here, brought me this far from the slums, the dingy little rooms and filthy men. You made me sorry for what I'd become, gave me a purpose for the first time in my life. I can't go away, Alan, not when you mean so much to me, not while you don't understand."

"I understand plenty."

Davon peered beyond him, through the porthole where distant stars and galaxies created a glow like sunlight seen from watery depths.

"Somewhere out there you and I will see things, learn secrets no one else has since the dawning of the universe." She shifted her gaze to his shadowy form. "I know you hate me right now. I know you think I let Juarez do what he did, but you won't be upset with me always. I can look ahead, see images through space dust. I see Faroul."

Their gazes met, and she went on. "You'll be there, Alan. You and me and somebody else."

Alan laughed cynically. "You can't see *anything*," he said angrily. "You were stuck in those ghettos so long the lemstel warped your mind. You started feeding me all these lines about how you can see things that haven't happened, know things that aren't. You think I believe that? All you can do is . . ."

He lowered his eyes, but his words already had cut through what little was left of her womanhood.

"Is . . . Is that how you really feel?" she asked. She started to slink away into the shadows, lose herself in her own fear and emotion, but then anger gripped her. "The first time I saw you, something happened to me. You made me feel like a person again. You stood up for me when nobody else would, seemed to care when others didn't. For the first time I began to know what it was like to be happy, to have somebody in all this madness that cared about me, wanted me for who I am inside."

"I suppose that's all Juarez wanted you for."

"No!" she cried, feeling her face flush. "It's a lie, all of it! It was for you, can't you see that? It happened before, right here, but I couldn't tell you. You would've tried to do something about it and he would've had you killed, just like that man in the commissary."

His voice seemed to lose all energy, all caring. "You don't have to do this, Davon. I trusted you, felt close to you, and then you let him take you like a thousand other men."

She started to lash out again, but his words hurt too much. "I . . . I thought you were different from the rest. I thought it didn't matter to you what I'd been. I . . . I guess I was wrong."

"Get out of here." He turned his back on her. "Go on back to him, let me die."

A sob crawled up from Davon's very soul. "If . . . If that's the way you want it, if that's all you care about me . . ."

She turned and walked away a couple of steps before looking back at him.

"I love you, Alan," she whispered. "No matter what you think of me, I love you."

The only response was the sound of her footsteps carrying her away.

Chapter Fifteen

Alan slept, and dreamed.

He stood on the edge of the great plains of Rhythia, and the night wind tousled his hair. He looked up at the stars crowding the sky, a hundred billion suns racing with infinite precision toward a predetermined destination.

His father was beside him suddenly, his young features without sign of aging. "What is it you're looking for, Alan? Tell me. Maybe I can help you."

Alan shook his head and seemed to feel the universe receding from his grasp. "No," he said quietly. "I can't have it. I can't have it ever."

His father's hand became tender on his arm and Alan looked into the intelligent eyes. Somehow they spoke of greater destinies than his own life or even his wildest dreams.

Alan felt a great sense of confusion. "You," he said, remembering the warheads strafing the planet. "You don't belong here."

His father's warm hand seemed to envelope him with strength, will. "You've got to fight, got to regain the will to live. We brought you this far, out of the mines, from the dead. We gave you the power. Why don't you use it?"

Alan frowned and tried to focus on the details of his father's face, but somehow they seemed vague, as if he were unable to interpret what he saw in terms of his own experiences.

"I don't understand, Father," he said. "You're here telling me this, but I saw the bombs fall, watched you die with our world."

The man pulled him close and embraced him. "Our world is everywhere, Alan. Here, there, wherever it takes us." He withdrew and looked directly into his son's eyes. "Don't lie there and die. You can't!

The universe depends on you. You've got to fight your pride, your bitterness, shove it out of the way.

"Fight, Alan, fight for Faroul! Blake Sharrel and Rhonda Gregory have already set it all in motion!"

Alan rolled over and felt the manacles bite his wrists. He groaned from deep inside and became aware of the ache in his muscles. He opened his eyes to darkness, yet his father's words still seemed distinct.

He shook his head and pulled himself up by the chains until he could rest his temples against a link. Why should he dream about his father after all these years? Why should words created by his subconscious send a tremor through him, leaving his mouth dry, his brow beaded with sweat like condensation on the frigid porthole?

Then other questions entered his mind, racing through maze-like. Indeed, why should he lie here and die? Why should the savage determination that had always ruled his life desert him now, when he needed it so desperately? Couldn't he summon perseverance from the depths of his will? Did he have to lie here passively accepting his own fate?

Father, what's wrong with me! Oh, Father, let me have a reason to live again, a will to keep fighting!

A thought detonated inside him like a dam crumbling to the force of a flood. He squeezed his fist and pulled himself to his feet, his teeth grinding, his arteries straining at their boundaries.

Faroul!

He pressed his face against the porthole and stared into the infinite reaches of space.

He had to make it! For himself! For his father! Because it was waiting for him!

He whirled to the crates that obliterated the light of the corridor. A guttural crawled up from his larynx. In an instant it metamorphosed into a savage cry that reverberated between the walls.

"Juarez!" he yelled. "A challenge! The airlock, for control of the ship, for Faroul!"

***

Juarez stood in the forward control deck picking his teeth with a small dagger. "You know," he said, looking up at Lindsay, "I always gave that friend of yours credit for having more sense."

Lindsay shrugged and glanced at the pirate with the severed ear who had relayed Alan's challenge. "He's at his rope's end. I don't think he feels he's got much choice."

Juarez laughed quietly. "Well, we'll see how he feels after rotting in those chains," he snarled, turning to walk away.

The other pirate became alert, frowning and taking a step toward Juarez. "Hey," he snapped, and abruptly all eyes were on him. "Way I remember it, if a man's challenged to the airlock, he fights. Or crawls back in his hole."

Juarez stiffened and whirled to level a vicious epithet at him. "You're treading on thin ice!"

Half Ear didn't seem fazed. He glanced at the other crewmen on deck. "A man who don't have guts enough to fight for the ship in the lock ain't staying in charge for long."

"Yeah," agreed the black Thalian, rising from his navigator's post. "It's always been that way in deep space. If a pirate can't stand up and defend his command in the airlock, he doesn't command."

Juarez turned crimson. "You call that a challenge for command? The scum's not even one of us! Suppose he did kill me—no way in hell—but say he did. You want an outsider who's never faced all the dangers that you have telling you what to do?"

"Maybe somebody better," said Half Ear. "Seems to me he did pretty well against that fleet of fighters. You sure as hell didn't."

Juarez went livid with rage, his beard twitching. "I'm in command of this ship! All you scum better respect me or I'll have you killed!"

He surveyed the men: the sunken eyes, scarred faces, merciless expressions. "If that dying old man wants to get himself killed, then bring the dog on! You think I'm scared of him? The only reason I kept him alive *this* long was because he knew Faroul's coordinates and we didn't. Now all of us know, and we're going there! If he's fool enough to want to die, throw him in the airlock so I can scatter his guts across the galaxy!"

***

Davon was in her secured cabin when she heard shouts ring out and boot heels meet floor, action replacing the dull routine of a starship. U.S.S. fighters? Poteet?

A sudden image of a cutlass dripping red with blood filled her mind, and then the perspective of her vision broadened and she saw the faces of Alan and Juarez.

No! She shook her head violently, trying to sweep away the images. Why was it *she* who had to see such things, be haunted by sights that never gave her peace? She didn't want to know, not before it happened, not ever.

She ran to the door and opened it. Crewmen scurried past, bound for a stairwell choked with men. Voices bartered for odds. Credits exchanged hands. And one after another the pirates descended toward the ship's lower reaches.

She rushed down the corridor, blood deluging her mind. What was happening? Why did she feel so ill at ease? What was it she perceived that never had been seen before, a ghastly vision that left her shaking uncontrollably?

She found Juarez descending out of sight, and then Lindsay appeared between levels. She despised him, but he seemed her only link to Alan, the only one she could reach out to for answers.

"Lindsay!"

She caught him just as his boots clanged against the metal rungs that would carry him to the level below. He turned, and they stood looking at one another through rails as though they were on opposites sides of a cell.

"It's Alan, isn't it?" she demanded. "What's happened to him?"

"It's not what's *happened*. It's what's about to."

"There's going to be blood," she stated with certainty. "Now tell me!"

Lines joined above the bridge of Lindsay's nose and he climbed toward her. "How do you know that?"

"You were like a son to him! Don't you remember? You've got to help him!"

Lindsay straightened. "How do you know so much? Who told you Alan and Juarez were going to fight in the airlock?"

Davon gripped the guard rail as if she were going to collapse. Her mouth went dry and her legs became like saplings in a gale. The airlock! He couldn't do it! The blood, it had to be his!

"You can stop it!" she pleaded. "For the love of God, you've got to do something!"

Lindsay started to reply, but the words vanished as soon as they came to his lips. He turned to descend, but then looked back at Davon looming over him. For the first time, she thought she could see a touch of concern in his face.

I . . ." He shook his head and ran his hand across his brow. "I wish it didn't have to be this way. But there's nothing I can do, no way to stop it."

To the sound of boots against rungs, he dropped out of sight.

In the years Davon had been trapped in the Thalian slums, she had heard grisly stories of how a pirate gained dominance over a ship by his prowess inside the airlock. It was a heartless battle that tested the physical, mental, and emotional abilities of the combatants, and she shuddered because Alan had no chance, not when the mines had taken so much from him.

The airlock, the exit and entry point for marauding pirates, lay outside the ship's gravitational system, creating a weightless environment supplied with oxygen. It was a large, well-lighted chamber, twelve meters long and half as wide and high, resembling in all aspects an ancient handball court such as still existed in trade centers. The outer wall was a glass portal, creating the impression that there was nothing to separate a person within from the glittering stars splashed like multi-colored jewels against blackness.

Placed inside the lock, allowed to float freely, would be two men, and a razor-sharp cutlass.

And only one would come out alive.

She had to stop it! No matter what Alan thought of her, she loved him and had to stop it!

The chamber lay deep in the hull on the starboard side, and Davon hurriedly descended to the proper level and followed the quickly assembled crowd through the oval passageway where voices and footsteps echoed cavern-like.

At the airlock hatch and adjacent corridor, pirates gathered like Romans in an arena. The dullness of many days of routine duty had given way to excitement. Bent fingers ran through greasy beards. Someone passed around a leche cigarette as smoke hugged the ceiling. The fates of two men's lives were bartered like double-beaked Rhythian cocks. While the majority of the credits was placed on Juarez, the tempting betting odds led several crewmen to overlook the savage beating Juarez had given Alan.

"Where is that pig?" bellowed Juarez. "Get that sick old man in here! Who was it bet on him? I'll cover anybody's credits, ten to one odds! I made him cower on the floor and this time I'll slit his throat!"

Someone brandished a cutlass at arm's length above the throng. It glinted in Davon's eyes and she stared at it, seeing blood that wasn't there stream down the blade like red banners. Then a crewmen unbolted the hatch and threw the weapon inside, where it twirled and floated away, alternately revealing its glittering point and steel handle.

Davon pushed her way through the crowd and sought out Lindsay. He stood beside Juarez with his back to her, holding the commander's credits, blue and orange strips of plastic in slender brown fingers.

She seized his arm and whirled him about. "What are you doing? It's Alan we're talking about. Don't you realize that? Did you pull him from those mines just to let him be butchered? Answer me!"

Lindsay's eyes widened and he looked down at her fingers sunk into his skin. He glanced apprehensively over his shoulder at Juarez, who had stepped away to loosen his muscles, and then faced her again.

"I . . . I told you I didn't want it this way," he said in a low monotone. He nodded to the crowding pirates. "What do you expect me to do? Look at them. This is what they want. *They want blood.* It's been too long since they've seen any. You think I can stop it?"

"You don't want to stop it! You just want Alan out of the way for good. Every time you see him you feel guilty for the way you've betrayed him!"

Lindsay jerked his arm free. "Get away from me!" he said, turning away.

***

They brought Alan up from the freight bay by way of the adjacent corridor. The manacles had painted red streaks in his wrists and there was a great weakness in his knees. Yet he felt grim determination, as if a ghetto-like toughness pervaded him.

His muscles had long-since atrophied. His once-formidable fighting skills had eroded like the hills he had helped carve away on Alos. All he had left was his will, and though he knew he faced certain death, he was glad for the chance to meet it as he had lived: by savagely attacking whatever stood in his way.

He saw Davon as he approached, and through the milling bodies their gazes met as they had light years away in a brothel bar. From the first, her eyes had captivated him, but now he saw in them only the reflection of his unattainable dreams, the crumbled hopes his pride had foredoomed.

A grim hush fell over the throng as Juarez confronted Alan with an intimidating stare, the veins in his thick neck bulging.

"I should've taken care of you a long time ago," Juarez snarled.

"Why didn't you?"

Juarez only glared.

"I'll tell you why," said Alan. "You pretend it was because of Faroul. The truth is, something inside of you makes you afraid of me."

"Afraid?" snorted Juarez. He glanced at the pirates. "This sick old man thinks I'm scared of him!"

Only silence.

"You're afraid," continued Alan, "because of what I was, because nobody else ever lasted nine years in the mines. You're afraid because you always knew I'd kill you."

Juarez's beard twitched. He whirled to the crew, his teeth gritted. "All you scum want me dead, don't you? You hate me, but I've kept you alive, filled your filthy pockets! Not you or that dog or anybody else can stop me!"

A pirate took a length of cord and tightly bound the two men, left wrist to left wrist with a meter's distance between. They started toward the airlock, and Juarez spun to Alan as they neared it.

"Let's get on with it. I got a whore to see!"

Alan looked back into Davon's eyes one last time and climbed through the hatch after Juarez.

Chapter Sixteen

Entering the airlock, going from a gravitational environment one moment to a weightless world the next, had no parallel in nature. It was both similar and dissimilar to stepping off a platform within watery depths. There was a sensation of being lifted upward by unseen hands, and then a sudden realization that there was no up or down, only here and there.

It created an impression of immense strength. No longer did Alan have to fight gravity to lift arm or leg, and his heart seemed more powerful, easily sending blood coursing through his body. Hair which usually had lain on head now streamed outward, and the loose uniform tossed with each movement, yielding contact with skin only when limb or torso pressed into it.

There was only an instant to become aware of all these things, for the pair was scarcely inside the chamber when a vicious fist struck Alan in the mouth, spewing blood to hang like drops of rain in the air.

Davon stifled a cry, and the hatch crashed shut.

Two men. Adrift in a sea of air. Bound together by hatred and a slender cord that snaked about, as if unsure which direction to fall.

And a single cutlass, its blade gleaming in the light like the scintillating stars through the glass portal.

Alan yanked violently on the cord. Body slammed against body as Juarez's forearm glanced off his ear. Alan drove a knee into the pirate's abdomen. The two became a tangled mass of pummeling arms, legs wrapping around calves, boots and elbows driving into cartilage. They twisted through open space, the constellations through the portal spinning before Alan's eyes. He could taste the sweat on Juarez's shoulders, smell his putrid breath.

Curses and groans rose up from deep inside as fists popped against cheek. Tiny droplets of blood danced before Alan and became fuzzy red balls as his forehead absorbed a stunning hook.

Stars and glimmering specks of silver swept through the chamber. The lights dimmed, and then brightened. Alan threw up an arm to fend off the blows that landed with sickening thuds against his skull. He felt himself drifting backward, tumbling crazily as in a dizzy fall in a nightmare.

The cutlass clanged against the portal and slowly rebounded toward them, but suddenly Juarez was behind him, gripping the cord tightly in his hands.

Alan kicked and tried to dodge. The cord scraped the hide on his chin and then slipped to his neck. His head went backward uncontrollably as nylon gouged his larynx. He gagged and desperately tried to dislodge it, but his fingers couldn't edge beneath. He squirmed like a mortally wounded animal in death throes as his tongue fell against the rear of his mouth.

He was dying! Air! He had to have air!

He reached back and grasped Juarez's hair, fighting to pull him off, but the pirate only tightened his hold.

Air! He couldn't breathe!

Blood filled Alan's forehead, creating immense pain as the arteries in his neck ceased to flow. No more! He couldn't take any more!

He crashed a savage fist into Juarez's head, and then again and again. His vision began to blacken, his arms and legs tingling strangely.

He couldn't do it! He was choking to death and he couldn't stop it!

In that brief moment in which he realized he was dying and that nothing in all the universe could change it, a peculiar image swept over him. It was not a picture of himself, kicking and squirming, or of Juarez suffocating the life from him. It was not even of Faroul, or the mystic old man whose words had led him to this.

It was only of Davon.

Davon!

He loved her! He loved her and now she would never know!

He felt his eyes bulge, saw his own sweat-streaked arm fighting at his throat, noticed the mysterious reaches of the galaxy beckoning beyond his boots. His strength fled, his willpower shattering from lack of oxygen. And yet he wasn't afraid. He was dying, and instead of the great fear he had held for it all his life, now that the time had come he no longer regarded it with horror and awe.

It was as if an immense tranquility overwhelmed him, obliterating all else, as if he slowly became one with the universe, with all that was calm and filled with purpose and meaning. He couldn't understand, and suddenly a light filled his senses, one as bright as an exploding nova. It seemed to come from an infinitely small pinpoint in the blackness beyond the portal, and then swarmed about him, its scintillating rays playing along his skin, infusing every cell with warmth, power, love.

Love. That was it. That was the feeling that emanated from it; that was the quality that created the unmistakable impression that the light was not a thing, but a person.

It was alive and was one with him, and for the first time in his life a true sense of happiness, beyond any conception he had ever had of the word, surged through him.

Help me! Whoever you are, give me the power to help myself!

The cutlass floated aimlessly ten meters away, and abruptly its blade caught his eye, the light dancing along its edge as if it were ablaze with power. As he watched, it slowly revolved until its point was a fiery pinhead against the ebony portal.

"Die!" cried Juarez. "Die!"

Alan saw it happen and somehow was not surprised, as if he stood and watched from beyond life's progression, knew things that he shouldn't have.

The cutlass moved toward them swiftly, not by change in the ship's course but as if by design, guided by powers beyond the physical.

"You're dead, you bastard!" cried the pirate.

Alan saw the blade swerve in mid-flight, and then he felt a shudder grip the man astride him, heard a sound like a kitchen knife slashing into a melon.

Juarez gave a long, terrifying cry that echoed from portal to wall. The cord went slack about Alan's neck. He drifted away, coughing and gasping for breath as he clutched his throat. Through the rope, grown taut, he felt the thrashing of the dying man, and when Alan turned, he saw a face contorted in agony, eyes wide but not understanding, to the last moment of life imploring the universe for answers.

Alan watched the squirms lessen, heard one last wheeze rise up, and then only utter stillness filled the man's frame. The body slowly began to revolve, the head dipping toward Alan's heels, the shoulder blades coming into view.

Buried midway between, leaving globules of blood drifting away, was the cutlass that never had been in Alan's grasp.

Alan pulled the corpse to him, feeling the stupendous awe of wonders beyond comprehension. He grasped the cutlass hilt and suddenly became aware that the being of light had vanished, as if it had receded into the starry expanse to become one with the myriad pinpoints of brightness.

He pulled the blade free with a sucking noise, and blood followed to become crimson snowflakes in the air. When he slashed the cord in half, Juarez's body, eyes staring but not seeing, slowly drifted away, revolving against the backdrop of a galaxy that somehow seemed to consume it.

Alan swam through open space and clanged on the hatch with the cutlass. Holding to a metallic protrusion as he heard the unbolting of the hatch, he looked back at the clouds of blood and cried out from deep inside for the love that he had felt in the presence of the being of light.

He longed for it as though there was nothing else in the cosmos. His innermost soul yearned for its warmth, as if he had lived all his life just to have communion with it. It defied logic, blasted the scientific knowledge imparted to him by the interstellar age. But it had been *real*, a person in whom he had felt totally at peace with himself and all of creation.

He stretched a blood-soaked hand toward the portal, imploring the being to take him with it, to surround him with the companionship that for a moment had filled the cavity inside him. He had to have it indwelling his very essence—forever.

The hatch screeched open, and a dozen stunned faces met his eyes.

***

During the eternity of minutes in which the hatch had been sealed, Davon had turned away to shiver and bury her face in her hands. She had just watched the one person who had ever brought her love and purpose crawl inside to die. She wandered aimlessly down the blurred corridor, her eyes stinging and an unbearable ache at the back of her neck. The salt grew bitter in her mouth, and she stopped to press her forehead into the wall. She put her fingers lightly against the metal, seeing her life and world as an empty, colossal joke, and the only reply as she cried for answers was the hollow echo of her own sobs.

She crashed her knuckles into the wall until they bled.

From down the corridor came voices, the kind that spawned a thousand questions, perpetuated enigmas. Davon brushed at her eyes and looked, finding a great milling of men. One sweaty arm rose above the rest, holding aloft a cutlass streaked with blood. The image filled her vision, captivated every cell in her mind, overwhelmed all other thoughts.

She followed the streaming rivulets down to hilt and fist, and then an abrupt shifting of pirates revealed shoulders, face, eyes.

Her hand came to her mouth, her breaths suddenly ceasing. A word played on her lips, summoned from deep within. In a whisper she voiced it: a name, *his* name.

Alan!

The floor seemed to collapse beneath her and she sank, sobbing unashamedly, the moisture gathering on the wall beside her.

***

Alan stood defiantly, letting the cutlass tower above the pirates as the blood ran down his arm.

"Look!" he shouted, and there was not another voice to be heard. "Look at the blood of Juarez! Look at the arm that now captains this ship!"

A pallor swept over the crewmen, even over those who had found the gambling odds too tempting and had bet against Juarez. Every eye was wide, as if trying through visual means to understand this inexplicable outcome.

Alan slowly turned about, his gaze penetrating as it met that of each pirate: the black and white, the earth stock and colonial half-breed. He had been in this situation before. He knew he was an outsider and had to gain their respect, show utter fearlessness, or he was already doomed.

"Now tell me!" he cried. "Tell me who rules this crew, or crawl through the hatch!" He looked at a slender Oriental a pace away. "How about you?" No reply. "Or you? Or you?"

One by one, he challenged them all.

The crewmen's stony silence was acquiescence enough, but it was up to the pirate with the severed ear to voice their affirmation. "Command's yours," he said, glancing about at nine menacing countenances and finding no one to dispute his words. "We all know how you saved the ship from those fighters. We know what you can do."

"Yeah," agreed the black Thalian, and a murmur of approval swept through the throng.

Alan looked about and found Lindsay trembling against the wall behind him. Their eyes merged and memories deluged Alan, images of a boy he had loved only to lose when U.S.S. authorities had separated them.

"You, Lin," he said quietly, his words suddenly hoarse. "What do you think?"

Lindsay opened his mouth to speak before hanging his head. He looked up and shrugged, a smile fighting its way onto his lips. "I . . . I'm glad you made it, Alan," he whispered.

Alan turned to survey the crew with close-set eyes.

"Okay!" he said, still brandishing the cutlass. "I captain this ship, nobody else! You do what I tell you and I'll keep you alive, keep your pockets lined with credits. But you do me wrong or steal from some other crewmen and the galaxy won't be big enough to hide in.

"Something else. Nobody touches the woman. The next port we make, you can have all the women you can buy, but while you're on my ship you'll do what I say. Now all of you want Faroul, think you're going to be like gods. Well, that's just where we're going. We're tracking down Poteet the same way I'll track down any of you that wrongs me."

Silence. And faces showing new-found respect born in part of fear.

Weak from the fight and no longer calling on adrenalin, Alan slipped the cutlass in his belt and turned to Lindsay. "Davon," he said simply.

The younger man shrugged. "She was here, then she walked away."

Alan started toward the main corridor, and the pirates cleared a path. He had gone only a few steps when he saw her slumped on the floor, twenty meters distant. He ran to her, his sudden sense of security shattering.

What had they done to her? In God's name, what had they done? He would have them killed! He would slay them with his bare hands!

He knelt beside her and placed a soft hand on her shoulder, feeling her tremble. "Davon?" His quiet voice was tentative, filled with worry, and he brushed away the hair so he could see her face. Her cheeks were as pale as moonlight through clouds. What was wrong? She *had* to be all right, had to because he realized now that he couldn't go on alone, that he would rather die than be without her.

"Davon!" Now there was urgency in his voice. He ran his fingers tenderly along her cheek, mouth, brow. The touch seemed to stimulate her, restore the color in her face, and she opened her eyes.

"Alan?" she whispered. "Are you here? Are you really here?"

He smiled and slipped an arm beneath her shoulders, then the other under the bend of her knees. "From now on."

With strength he didn't know he had, he lifted her in his arms, and she responded by curling her hands about his neck and snuggling her face against his chest.

Chapter Seventeen

Alan carried Davon to his quarters as her mind overflowed with all sorts of longings and questions. She clung to him quietly, delighting in the sensation of his body warm against hers.

In his cabin he dimmed the harsh lights so that the shadows were heavy, and laid her gently on the jet mattress. She looked up at him, not wanting to disengage her arms. For a moment he stared at her, and then he ran his fingers lightly along her red-tinged cheeks. Never before had she seen him so gentle, so concerned. Drying blood caked the back of his hand and he withdrew, nodding to the Catholian Ray booth a few meters away.

"I've got to clean up," he whispered.

Her soft hands played along his shoulders, arms, fingers as he pulled away. He hesitated, looking down at her, and Davon felt something reawaken inside her, as if his touch had made her alive again.

Finally he slipped away to cleanse himself and change clothes, and Davon was alone to think and remember.

She pressed her cheek into the pillow, feeling it cool against her skin. She remembered how she had seen him in a vision, a proud and defiant man. Then their eyes had met in the boisterous tavern and her life had never been the same. Shame had replaced the instinct for survival that had driven her to the brothels, and the new hope that had dawned in his presence had helped ease her guilt.

She loved him! She loved him and wanted his arms about her forever, as if she had never lived for any other reason.

She closed her eyes and her dreams carried her afar, to a land and an event beyond anything she had ever known. When she opened them again Alan was easing down beside her, the freshness of his skin like sun-dried honey.

He supported himself with one hand, and with the other he caressed her silky hair, her forehead, cheeks. Davon took his fingers, kissing the bruises, the cuts in the knuckles, as his eyes spoke words more meaningful than any she had ever heard. When he lay beside her, she rested her head on his shoulder and ran her fingers through his hair. His lips found her mouth, and the kisses quenched the needs of a person who had gone so long without love.

They lay entwined in each other's arms for a long time, each of them exploring the tenderness and care in every touch, every expression. Only now did Alan speak the words she had already read in his eyes.

"I love you, Davon. I . . . I need you. Forever."

She smiled and embraced him as though she would never let go. "Forever," she whispered.

But then a sudden awe seemed to overwhelm him. "Something happened to me in there," he murmured. "Something I can't explain, don't understand."

Davon withdrew far enough to find his features hinting at mysteries. "Tell me, because there's not you and me anymore, there's us."

Sitting up, he stared into the shadows. "It was like I'd never lived before. I was dying, sorry I'd never told you how much I cared, and it saved me."

Perplexed, she came to her elbow so that his eyes focused on her again. "What saved you? How? How could you have killed Juarez?"

He breathed deeply, as if appreciating air and life as never before. He brushed back her hair. "You," he whispered. "You've talked about your faith, experiencing a light that gave you power."

She anticipated, beginning to understand. "It came to you, didn't it?"

He looked beyond her, his eyes assuming a faraway, dreamy look. "It happened before, in the mines. But this was different, something more." He peered into her eyes again. "It was a being, a person who seemed so full of love for me that I never wanted to leave it. I just wanted to bathe in its warmth, its presence, its companionship. Juarez had wrapped the cord around my neck, strangling me, and there was no way in the universe to keep from dying.

"Then suddenly it was there—no, *he*—and I didn't feel afraid anymore, didn't even feel anger at Juarez, just an indescribable feeling of love. The cutlass was clear across the airlock, then it wasn't. One moment it was floating, then the next it plunged into his back.

"What can it mean, Davon? What in Heaven's name can it mean?"

She hugged him close, sharing in some small degree his brush with eternity, and her tears wet his face and neck. "It means," she sobbed softly, "that it's not an accident you're still alive, that it was never an accident you came into the world."

And like the first primeval pair on a planet whirling about a distant star, man and woman found solace in each other's arms.

***

And so Alan came to rule an interstellar ship hurtling at tremendous speed through the enigmatic void of space, at his command a savage hybrid of modern-day buccaneers, crooks, and thieves who respected his ferocity and intelligence. Only a short time before, he had been a U.S.S. captive doomed to work the mines until he died, but through perseverance and something more, he had risen to the heights and gained a sense of purpose beyond conception.

The day after the battle Lindsay caught him on the forward control deck, where he stood before star clusters that sped toward them yet never seemed to shift positions. Charts rustled in Alan's fingers as he studied them intently.

"Alan?"

Alan lowered the charts and turned. For the first time since troops had dragged them in separate directions all those years ago, he felt the confidence that commands respect and lures others into following.

"Lin," he said warmly. He nodded to the swivel chairs at the navigator's post. "Let's sit down, talk a minute."

Lindsay hesitated. "I thought maybe you didn't want to have anything more to do with me."

Alan frowned. "What are you talking about?" He motioned with his head. "Come on over here."

They sat. Lindsay ran his fingers along the chair's leathery edge. "I guess Davon probably told you a lot of things about me," he said, his voice barely louder than the computers.

"No, she hasn't told me a thing since long before I went down to Myolia III." He noted the way Lindsay's eyes were glassy and blood-shot. "You've been drinking lemstel a lot, haven't you?"

The younger man shrugged. "I guess you know me better than anybody. From the time I was little, you always knew when something was bothering me, even if I didn't know it myself." He lowered his head. "I don't have to say anything about the way I've acted, the things I've said, since we got involved with Juarez. I . . . I guess you feel like I haven't done you right, stood up for you the way I should have."

Alan looked at him a long while, and when he finally spoke, his words were reserved, carefully chosen. "Is that what *you* think?"

Lindsay sighed deeply and stood, turning away. He walked a few meters and stopped before the observation porthole, pressing his hand against its smoothness. "Maybe I'm still just a scared little boy. Maybe I don't have what it takes to be a man, to stand up no matter what might happen to me. Maybe I should be like you. But I can't help it, Alan. There's so many different things jumbled up inside me, so many things telling me do this or that. It's like I'm somebody I don't even know."

Alan rose and went to him, putting his hand on his shoulder. For the first time since he had recognized him on Alos, he felt Lindsay needed him. "Don't worry about it, Lin. It's hard sometimes to know what the best thing to do is."

Lindsay turned, and abruptly it was as if nothing had ever changed between them, as though it were ten years earlier. Without shame Alan hugged him, and the stars through the porthole became fuzzy silver balls.

"We'll make it, Lin," he muttered, his love for the younger man deluging him with memories. "And don't tell me you don't have what it takes to be a man. You got me out of Alos, risked your neck to get me out of hell. Nobody but a man could've done that."

They disengaged and the lines at Lindsay's eyes spoke eloquently. "I'm sorry for the way it's looked," Lindsay said with cracked voice. "But I want you to know that from here on out I'm with you all the way, no matter what."

Alan smiled and clasped his hand tightly. "That's all I could ask of anyone. Now why don't we forget all this, start thinking about what we've got to do."

Lindsay raised an eyebrow. "You know, I've learned a lot about communications and computer analysis since I've been onboard. If I can help the crew along those lines . . ."

Alan patted him on the shoulder, his pride for the younger man showing. "You bet. We'll make it, Lin. We'll get Poteet, won't we?"

Lindsay smiled as a son does to his father and walked away.

***

The ship continued to plummet onward through largely unexplored space toward the galaxy's outer fringes, where the spiral arms of the Milky Way slung millions of stars on an epochal journey about the galactic center. Long ago, unmanned U.S.S. probes had been dispatched to gather data on radiation and other phenomena, but findings had been withheld by a governmental hierarchy that decreed all areas beyond the colonies forbidden.

Yet, others had defied the order before, but it had been up to a wizened old man with a messianic following to return alive, a perishing shell with esoteric stories of awesome, unleashed energy in a land bearing Hebraic inscriptions.

Faroul was ahead somewhere, its mysteries getting ever-closer, while familiar worlds receded like a coastline to the earliest oceanic venturers.

The tedious routine of an interstellar craft was not interrupted for a long while after Alan assumed command. The pirates afforded him the respect due a leader, like a wolf pack obligingly following the strongest in a frenzied chase across a moonlit ice pack. They obeyed his orders, listened quietly when he spoke, and offered none of the mutinous characteristics that could lead to violence.

But there were times—moments in which they believed him preoccupied—that he would catch them staring at him, as if to say to themselves, what is *he* doing captaining us? How could he possibly have slain Juarez, he, just a fragile old man who had bled at the pirate's feet?

He would discern the glances at the meal table, or on the forward control deck or lower observation port. And then the eyes quickly would shift, as if the strange circumstances that had brought him into leadership were something to fear.

Alan spent his free moments continuing to discover in Davon an entirely different person from the one he had known. He pondered the matter a great deal, and then a solemn realization dawned on him that it was not she who had changed, but he. An indefinable quality, long submerged or forgotten, had crept back into his character. From the night he had held Davon in his arms and told her of his love, he never again had dwelt on what had happened with Juarez in her cabin.

It didn't matter anymore. He didn't care what she had done, how much she had betrayed his trust. He had difficulty summoning up any emotion other than love, so vivid was the memory of the being of light. Too, he found himself calmly accepting Lindsay's statement of regret, despite all that had gone on before.

But his newfound disposition began to fade even as Davon pointed out that something had metamorphosed in him.

They sat at a table on the dining deck, eschewing manufactured food in favor of Thalian eggs, Altarian hare, and vegetables from the Rhythian asteroid belt. It was late and only a couple of crewmen remained: one in the corner sipping lemstel, the other at the porthole devouring meat with greasy hands.

"You've changed, Alan," she said quietly, her elbow brushing his arm. "You're different somehow, ever since . . ."

He looked at her, the events in the airlock alive in his memory. "Is that good or bad?" he joked.

She smiled, put her hand inside his arm, and leaned close. "I'd never seen anybody so full of hate. All you could talk about was getting back at the United Star Systems and Poteet. I could see it tearing you apart, piece by piece. The bitterness was in your eyes, but now it's faded."

Alan breathed deeply and felt his fork with his fingertips. "No, it's still there, deep inside, coming back more and more all the time." He put his hand on hers. "For a day or two, it was like all the evil ideas and desire for revenge were squeezed out. I was so caught up in all the joy and love that nothing else mattered. I couldn't even muster any hatred for Poteet, wondered why I'd ever want to kill him."

He looked down at his platter. "But now those feelings are starting to rub off. Back in the airlock, there was nothing in the universe I wanted to do besides be with that being, as if it was the only reality there was. But the longer I go without it, the more I start retreating to the old desires, the hate."

Her comforting fingers brushed his cheek. "Don't worry about it," she whispered. "The feelings and memories might dim, but they'll never go away."

He looked at his pale hands. "No," he agreed, "I won't forget, never stop wishing it had taken me with it."

"Did you tell Lindsay?"

He looked up at her and a smile creased his face. "Lin. Now there's a boy I thought I'd lost. But you know what? I saw him on the forward control deck and we talked just the way we used to when he was a kid. He really loves me, Davon, no matter what he's done before. He told me he was sorry, that from here on out I can count on him."

Davon looked away, and for a long while there was only the belching of the crewman who quaffed lemstel. Finally her bosom rose and she surveyed Alan gravely.

"Maybe I shouldn't say anything like this," she began hesitantly, "but are you sure about Lindsay? Are you sure he's not just jumping on the bandwagon because—"

"No!" Alan exclaimed angrily. "I know him! I raised him like my own son! Don't you think I know a little about him?"

Hurt filled Davon's features. She started to respond, but turned and slowly stood. She went to the door, a sob in her throat and her hand a veil over her eyes, and looked back at him.

"I . . . I'm sorry, Alan," she whispered, and continued through the door.

"Davon, I . . ."

But no, Alan's regret refused to be expressed, no matter how much a part of him wanted to voice it.

Chapter Eighteen

The day before the ship was to enter the globular cluster that harbored Faroul, a new mystery flared, one Alan instantly recognized as a sign of something other than the total allegiance a crew should afford its captain.

He had descended to the lower hull to make a routine inspection of the central computers. Under Juarez's command, he had never been allowed access to the cramped chamber guarded by safety control mechanisms, for here lay the very heart of the ship. The master computer and lesser ones worked constantly, clicking, humming, vibrating as they maintained the craft's systems: engine, life support, gravitational, even food production.

He sat on a stool before a monitor, a wireless ear phone in place as he reviewed post-light communications from the memory banks. It was almost time for the meal summons and he was growing weary of the standard intercepted messages from U.S.S. starships and bases. His stomach growled and he shifted uncomfortably, and then a series of red digital lights flashed across the screen.

He frowned and leaned forward to rewind the tape. It squealed like a thousand high-pitched voices before clicking to a stop. Pressing the start button, he replayed the last few minutes. Standard intercepts. Verbal readouts of coordinates. Typical subspace and post-light chatter.

And something else.

Parading across the screen, as if painting a marquee, were colorful numbers.

Blood coursed through his arteries, and he ran a parallel check on the instrument panel. Still the same. Coded messages had been relayed weeks before. He took out a note pad and copied them, noting the dates.

As a young officer in the U.S.S., he had studied every code system in use; this, however, he could not decrypt, as if someone deliberately had transmitted signals that others would be unable to understand.

Why would Juarez have dispatched messages? With whom in all the empire could he have had allegiance, he, a merciless pirate who had given the impression of having no interaction with other pirate bands?

It mystified Alan. As he continued to review tapes at an increased rate of speed, he discovered that an entire series of such numbers had been transmitted at regular intervals, the last of which had been *two hours after Juarez had died.*

Alan's impulse was to inquire of the crew. But his pirates were only a few days' removed from being his foes, and furthermore, the use of cryptology was an obvious attempt at secrecy.

Secrecy. Betrayal. Mutiny. They followed one another as logically as death succeeded life.

The dinner call sounded, and as Alan stuffed his notes inside his shirt, he knew that danger lurked as surely as a cutlass against his heart.

Later in the shift he found Lindsay in the lower observation area, a snout-shaped deck with floor, ceiling, and three walls of interstellar-age glass for optimum visual purposes during battle. As Alan stepped through the hatch, he was overwhelmed by the sensation that he was apart from the ship, floating freely through the universe and separated from anything man had ever touched. Far-flung star fields seemed mere specks in an all-encompassing infinity that swallowed his self-identity.

A tingle, then a brief shudder, swept through his frame. What was it about the mysterious reaches that made him feel this way? He had once served two months in the lower observation area of a U.S.S. star-ship, yet he had never experienced such a sensation. Was there really something different about the deck this time? Or was there an indefinable factor within himself that made him view things differently and grasp for answers in face of enigmas?

He walked up and stopped beside Lindsay, who stood staring through the side porthole where condensation beads streamed down.

"Alan," said the younger man. "You slipped up on me. Didn't know anyone else was around."

"There may be too many around."

Lindsay obviously didn't pick up on Alan's concern, for he nodded to the globular cluster that had grown ever brighter over the last several hours. "I was just wondering what's out there. Looks like it won't be long now till we know."

Alan looked. The cluster seemed to loom like a thousand sparkling jewels floating on a sea of darkest indigo. "No, it won't be long," he agreed. Then he surveyed the younger man. "But then maybe it's already been forever."

Lindsay frowned. "What's that mean?"

Alan shook his head and ran his fingers along his pants leg. "Lin, I've got this funny feeling in the pit of my stomach that I've wasted my whole life when I should have been *there*." He nodded to the cluster. "It's like I tried doing things on my own all these years, and now a force beyond my understanding's behind it all."

Lindsay rasped a hand across his bristly face. "I think you're talking way above my head, like you used to when you'd try to explain nuclear energy to me."

Alan's chest expanded and he smiled. "Yeah," he said quietly. "But you know, Lin, there's just so many things nobody understands, about the universe, about themselves. Look at us a minute. Here we are in a one-hundred meter starship and we're just a speck compared to all the star systems in the U.S.S. And yet the whole empire is like a grain of sand compared to the vastness you see out there. We're *nothing*, so small, insignificant, yet . . ."

He glanced at the galaxy's outer reaches that formed a cloud sweeping through the heavens. "It's like I suddenly feel we're going to do something to change it, to affect it in a way that's never been done before in all eternity."

Lindsay smiled. "You've been reading too much science fiction," he said, laughing. "The truth is, there's really not much we *can* do to affect anything. The universe has been around for billions of years, stars forming, dying, and I imagine it'll keep right on doing it until—"

"That's something that's always bothered me," interrupted Alan. "Until what?" He motioned to the massive cluster ahead, and beyond to the spiral formations of distant galaxies and galactic clusters. "Look at all that. All those specks, those clouds made up of billions of stars each. Think of all the energy each one is expending, shooting across galactic emptiness, the eons it's taken those light rays from other galaxies to get this far."

He found Lindsay's eyes. "Remember when you were a kid, the way you buried your nose in all those books on thermodynamics?"

Lindsay laughed. "How could I forget? You just about crammed them down my throat."

Alan smiled. "Maybe I knew I'd be old and forget all that stuff someday, like now. Why don't you refresh my memory on thermodynamics, the law of entropy increase."

Lindsay scratched his head and grinned. "You never forget anything. Okay, as I remember it, in any energy transfer or change, although the total amount of energy remains the same, the degree of usefulness, availability, is always lessened."

Alan put his hand on the younger man's shoulder, and there was a measure of pride in the gesture. "Sounds like you're talking above *me* now," he commented. Then his expression turned solemn. "In other words, in any closed system—the universe included—the overall energy is constantly being degraded as long as there's any energy transfer at all."

"What brings all this on?" asked Lindsay. "Yeah, you always lose some of the usable energy because it's dissipated in non-recoverable friction or heat."

Alan nodded as he turned to the porthole. "I see," he said quietly. "That means the universe is winding down." He looked into the younger man's face. "It's *dying*, because it's losing energy at an astounding rate every second, on all levels from biological actions to nuclear transformations inside stars."

"I guess you could put it that way."

Alan fixed his gaze on the massive cluster that raced toward them at breakneck speed. "Lin, if it's growing old, what happens at the end?"

Lindsay shook his head. "I don't guess anything does. It would be a dead universe, completely without life or energy or light, just nothing but masses in a void. Not much use worrying about it, though. It can't take place for who knows how many billions of years. And what do we know? Maybe there's a built-in system somewhere out there to perpetuate it, like steady-state creation. Or maybe it'll just all blow up one of these days and start over again. What brought all this on, anyway?"

Alan pressed his hand against the porthole, feeling the moisture trickle down his palm. "It's dying. *We're dying*. But who could save it, even if he wanted to?" His voice was quiet, his tone speaking of great mysteries, the enigma of life itself.

Lindsay readjusted his belt and glanced toward the hatch. "Well, think I'll go catch some rest. I want to be awake when we enter the Faroul system."

"Wait a minute, Lin, before you run off." Alan edged nearer and his voice became quieter. "I wanted to catch you alone, clue you in."

Lindsay raised an eyebrow. "Something wrong?"

Alan rubbed the back of his neck. "Earlier in the shift I was running routine checks in the computer center, came across a bunch of coded transmissions."

Lindsay knitted his brow. "Standard intercepts?"

"No. These were encrypted unlike any I've ever seen."

"I don't understand."

Alan shook his head. "I don't either. You know, when it comes down to it, you're the only one besides Davon I can trust. You got this whole thing set up. What do you know about Juarez? He mixed up with any other pirate bands? Have dealings with black marketers on the other side of the empire?"

Lindsay shrugged. "He was just a two-bit pirate somebody in the black market led me to. I don't have any idea who he'd be sending transmissions to."

"That's just it. Apparently he's not the only one. That last transmission went out a couple of hours after he was dead."

Lindsay stiffened. "My Lord, Alan, you don't think somebody's planning a mutiny."

"I don't know *what* to think unless I can decrypt the stuff. And who could the messages have been sent to anyway, way out in deep space? By the time that last transmission went out, we were thousands of light years past the last outpost."

He produced a slip of paper from his shirt and extended it to the younger man. "Here, dabble with it, see what you can come up with. But for Heaven's sake, Lin, don't let anybody catch you with it. I've seen enough blood spilled on this ship already."

The paper rustled in Lindsay's fingers as he looked it over. "I'll take it to my bunk, get started on it right away." He turned and started to the hatch.

"Hey, Lin."

Lindsay paused and looked back.

"I hope to God you can figure something out," said Alan. "I wish to God somebody could tell me what all this means, explain all the images and thoughts jumbled up inside me."

As Lindsay continued through the hatch, Alan turned again to the approaching cluster and wondered if any of the answers awaited him there.

Chapter Nineteen

The moment the intercom announced the approach of the ship to the Faroulian system and deceleration to sub-light speed, Davon felt a pronounced unease. She stopped in the corridor outside her cabin and put her hand to her head, trying to force away an intense ache.

Then, like waves lapping planks and beams of a broken ship onto shore one at a time, the images came. Empty space flaring into a maelstrom of fiery gases, crimson and blue. Streaming projectiles illuminating blackness like tracers of cannon fire in the night. Bodies slamming into portholes, being crushed beneath girders. A score of men screaming, bursting.

And just beyond, a flaming sea that did not consume.

Danger! Danger and annihilation lurked nearby!

Fear swept over her like a billowing storm cloud. Alan! No matter their exchange over Lindsay, she needed him to hold her close and tell her not to be afraid, tell her that everything was as it should be. But it wasn't; something was going to happen!

She shook off the images and hurried to the forward control deck. The moment she stepped through the hatch, the glare of an immense sun sent specks dancing before her eyes. She shaded her brow and found virtually the entire crew gathered, drawn by greedy anticipation.

The craft veered and the sun sank like a ship sailing beyond the horizon across a sea of indigo. Distant stars glittered like a million neon lights on parade. Suspended as if by invisible strings were bloated ellipsoids of red giants, pinpoint double stars and triple systems, gleaming gases spewing from solar eruptions, and huge clouds of dust that left gaping holes in the heavens. For a moment, the ship seemed bound for a dwarf star in a doughnut of bluish gas. Then the ship completed its course change and a planet suddenly filled the entire porthole and widened Davon's eyes.

Red, splotched with blue, met her gaze. *Déjà vu* overcame her. *Yes!* She had been here before, a thousand times in her mind.

***

Before the porthole, Alan sat at the master controls, watching the panorama of a vast uncharted land sweep below as the computers brought the ship into a one thousand-kilometer orbit about the planet.

Abruptly it seemed as if there were only he and the world before him in all of creation. *Faroul!* His fingers clawed at the porthole as if seeking to reach out and seize the eerie landscape of blue clouds, brown land masses, and immense red sea that wasn't a sea.

I've come! You kept me alive, pulled me out of hell, brought me clear across the galaxy. What is it you want? What do you want from me?

Everyone else seemed equally awestruck. It was unspeakable, how vastly different a world this seemed from any they had ever known. Swirls of blue, like gigantic hurricanes, raced across misty seas tinted like a Martian sunset. But the colors were not constant, the hues deviating from orange to pink, blue to sapphire; indeed, the entire planet seemed to pulsate like an unstable ball of energy ready to explode.

"We're in orbit," said the navigator.

Lindsay rushed forward and stopped at Alan's elbow. "Is that it, Alan?" he panted, voicing the same question that likely was in everyone's mind. "Is that Faroul?"

Alan relaxed his hands and eased back in his chair. "He tried to tell me about it," he whispered. "He tried to describe it, but who could ever make somebody understand what *that* was like? It's never the same from one second to the next."

Alan turned to the Thalian who sat two meters away. "What kind of readings you get? The chemical makeup, density?"

The crewman scanned the instrument panel and pushed a series of buttons. "What the—" He shifted uneasily and repeated the procedure. "The scanners, something's wrong with 'em."

"What do you get?"

"Atmosphere's breathable, oxygen, helium, nitrogen, but that sea. The computers can't even register its composition. It's not—what in hell—not hydrogen, hasn't even evolved *that* far."

"That doesn't make sense," said Alan, jumping up to view the panel for himself. "Hydrogen's the most basic element there is."

"Not anymore," said the Thalian. "That sea's made up of something smaller than electrons. I—" He started, slinging a hand toward a readout. "My God, its mass! It's so far off the scale the instruments can't even read it."

Lindsay was beside them. "This thing can compute masses of entire *galaxies*," he blurted. "Malfunction. Got to be."

Alan stared at the world as they sped into the sunset, where an eerie orange glow lighted the nocturnal sea. "Maybe," he said quietly. Then he looked at the younger man. "Or maybe you're looking at what you came for"—he faced the rest of the crew—"what all of you came for."

He nodded to the planet. "Look at it. That's what you wanted, isn't it? We may be orbiting above a world with a mass greater than a billion galaxies, just sitting there waiting for God to explode it like He did in the creation.

"Well, isn't that what you want? To play God?" He laughed contemptuously. "The hell you will!"

A tempestuous silence reigned over the confused faces and wide eyes, a silence that threatened to detonate.

Lindsay leaned close to his ear. "Don't tell them that, Alan," he pleaded. "They're on edge, full of anticipation. They've just risked their necks coming thousands of light years for Faroul. Don't tell them now they can't have it."

***

Davon had stood captivated as the frightening visions kept gnawing at her like an arctic storm. She went toward Alan and stared at the sea of scarlet and lapis lazuli that seemed to reach out for her, drowning her very essence in its depths.

It's you! You're what's haunted me all my life!

And now they were headed for it, on a rendezvous course with a force greater than all of them, more powerful than the United Star Systems or a hundred billion warheads.

She put a hand on his shoulder and he turned. "Davon," he said quietly. He nodded to the world, where night became aglow with the radiance of the sea. "Whatever it is that's out there, whatever destroyed Kasterfayette because he lost it, it looks like we're going to find out soon."

Davon motioned to the hatch. "I've got to tell you something," she said hurriedly.

Alan took her arm and they quickly crossed the deck and stopped at the hatch. "What's wrong?" he asked.

Her hand went to his shoulder. "I'm afraid, Alan. I've seen something that scares me."

"Tell me."

"It's like some kind of explosion . . . fire, something nobody expects, like—"

"Burke! Something's pulled into orbit right behind us!"

***

Alan spun to the Thalian across deck. "What are you talking about?"

"Screen shows a ship, forty kilometers behind us, closing fast!"

A ship! Out here in no-man's land, in unexplored space!

Alan's throat went dry. Poteet! It had to be Poteet! He rushed to the navigator's post and leaned over his shoulder to see the grid and the white dot that traced a direct course for them.

"What is it?" exclaimed Lindsay.

Alan made a fist. "I told you he'd be here!" He pivoted to the crewmen who milled in confusion. "Everybody to battle stations! If it's Faroul you want, you'll have to fight like hell to get it!"

In a moment the ship was in an uproar. Men rushed through the hatch to assume posts in the lower observation deck and engineering and life support areas. Alan hurried to the main controls to watch the blip dance across a separate screen. Lindsay spun one way, then another, before taking position at the communications post. Davon stood watching helplessly.

"He's trying to come up on us broadside!" exclaimed Alan. "Change the lay of the ship zero point one three. Keep our tail to him!"

The navigator locked in the course change as the radio crackled with a report from the lower observation deck.

"Two warheads, three o'clock!"

"Brace yourselves!" yelled Alan.

He heard Davon's gasp and Lindsay's curse, and he gritted his teeth, real fury surging through him for the first time since the airlock.

A missile streaked by, a burst of fiery gases, and then came a second, this one so close that Alan could see the O-rings defining the stages.

"Bring us around so the bogie's visible in the porthole!" ordered Alan. "I want to see the whites of his eyes before we blow him to hell!"

Centrifugal forces threw him off-balance. The sweeping porthole changed colors, from the crimson of the planet to blackness punctuated with stars, and then a bright metallic object appeared like the glint of sunlight from a distant mirror.

"Come on, you swine!" challenged Alan, watching the speck grow in size. "Let's do it, once and for all!" He turned to the crewman at his left. "Lock in the starboard warheads on that ship! Fast!"

Got it!" cried the pirate.

"Fire one, two, three!"

A multitude of memories swarmed through Alan as he watched the missiles streak outward, three trails of bluish and orange fire slashing through space. Even with his naked eye he could see the enemy ship take evasive action. Then warheads were screaming toward his own craft, a dozen multi-colored streams of potential death forming a shotgun-like pattern above the planet.

"Shift zero point two three!" he ordered. "Fire the port warheads!"

Tense moments seemed an eternity as Alan sat helplessly watching the missiles converge on them. It had to be Poteet! Who else in the galaxy would draw upon Alan's own tactic of scattering a dozen warheads along a ship's course? No matter how a ship dodged, one missile was still likely to hit home.

"Missiles at two o'clock!" cried a crewman from the lower observation deck. "They're coming right at us!"

"Full speed, zero point two five!" commanded Alan. He spun to see Davon at the hatch. "Get down! Hang on to something!"

He saw her drop, and suddenly everything about him convulsed as though by earthquake.

"We're hit!" someone cried over the radio. "Lower aft hull!"

"Seal the aft hatches!" directed Alan.

"Warhead!" screamed another voice. "It's lodged in the main nuclear engine, waiting to go off!"

"Good God!" yelled Lindsay. "We're going to blow!" He leaped toward Alan and seized his shoulder. "Do something! You've got to do something!"

Alan shoved him. "Out of my way!" He leaned into the microphone. "Give me the extent of damage to those engines!"

"I can't tell! That thing's just stuck through the hull staring at me! We're losing power; the pressures dropping down here!"

"Get out of there!" shouted Alan. "Seal all the hatches up to level two!"

"Central life support's failing!" came another report. "Extensive structural damage to the lower hull!"

"Give me a report on those last warheads we fired!" said Alan.

"They evaded them! Maybe a minor hit, nothing more!"

"Fire the starboard warheads, then the port ones; create a scatter zone ten kilometers wide!"

Fingers pressed buttons, slammed levers into console. "They're on their way—wait, something else! We've got another wave of missiles coming at us!"

Alan clenched his fists and his blood ran hot in his forehead. "He doesn't care anymore!" he cried. "He knows Faroul's down there and he's willing to stand and trade potshots! If he can't have it, he's going to make sure nobody else can either!"

He pivoted to Davon, who huddled beside the hatch. "So you saw us on Faroul." He nodded to the porthole, where a score of warheads sped toward them. "I wish you'd been right."

"Three missiles zeroed in on the enemy craft!" shouted the navigator.

Alan whirled to see an explosion against the distant ship, then another and another like lights flashing in the night.

"We got him!" he yelled. "We got that swine good!" He turned to the navigator. "The scanners, what do they show?"

The Thalian surveyed instruments. "Looks functionally dead. Wait, looks like . . ."

Alan went to his side to see the grid for himself. "A shuttle craft," he said, gritting his teeth. "Damn! He's getting away in a shuttle craft!"

"Somebody is, that's for sure," said the Thalian. "Scanners show the ship's life support system gone. It's just a floating wreck, space debris."

"What the hell about us?" exclaimed Lindsay, almost maniacal fear in his voice. He seized Alan's arm and spun him about. "We're going to blow! We're all going to die and you're just standing there!"

Alan fended off Lindsay's hand and shook him by the shoulders. "Shut up! You hear me, Lin? Shut up! We *will* die if you keep running around screaming we are. Now get out of here!"

Alan pivoted to the radio. "Give me a report on that warhead!"

"Thing could blow any second!" came a frantic reply. "It'll set off a chain reaction in the nuclear generators and blow us so far that even hell won't be able to find us!"

"My God!" came another voice over the radio. "We'll all be killed! Our only hope's the shuttle!"

Then came curses, the sound of a struggle that culminated with Banning fire that set the radio crackling with static.

Alan spun, his eyes first meeting the Thalian's, then Lindsay's. A frigid sweat broke out on his face, for in each he saw the same thing: a mad desire to stay alive at any cost, no matter who they had to kill.

The Thalian's eyes blazed as his fingers trembled along his Banning strap, and for a protracted moment he and Alan just stared at one another. Then the Thalian was on his feet, staging a frantic race with Lindsay for the hatch.

"No!" shouted Alan.

He dived after the Thalian, catching his ankle and bringing him down. Alan rolled over to see fingers withdraw the Banning, its barrel a pinpoint of darkness before his face, and then Davon cried out and enemy missiles rocked the ship with the fury of a volcanic eruption.

The force of the impact shook the weapon free. It clanged to the floor beside the hatch. Alan drove a fist into the pirate's face and absorbed a crushing elbow to his ribs. The next thing he knew, the Thalian had lifted a cutlass, its blade gleaming in the overhead lights as it flashed downward.

Alan's hand met the man's wrist. The point slashed his forearm, and then Davon lunged for the Banning and found it. As the struggle for the cutlass continued, Alan saw her level the weapon on the pirate and squeeze the pressure release. It exploded like lightning, and Alan rolled the dead Thalian off him and seized the cutlass.

"Let's go!" he yelled, gaining his feet and taking her arm. "They'll be trying for the shuttle! It's our only chance!"

As they ran through the hatch, Alan felt the warmth of her hand and found inner strength, a new will to live, a new desire for Faroul.

Faroul! That was it! That was what made him keep going, running down corridors, descending stairs with heaving lungs and a pain in his side!

They met a pirate coming from the corridor on the fourth level. The man saw the Banning in Davon's hand and went for his own. Alan saw that she would never react in time and dragged her down to the steps with a cry.

A bolt of energy streaked by, searing the wall and raising a stench. Rolling to his elbow, Alan took the Banning from her and leveled it on the pirate through the guard rail. The man dived out of sight, cursing viciously. Then a commotion caught Alan's attention from the stairway above, and he looked to see another pirate descending with raised cutlass.

The first pirate fired again, singeing Alan's hair, and when Alan glimpsed the assailant he squeezed off a bolt that caught the shooter in the chest.

Almost simultaneously, Davon gave a cry of warning. Whirling, Alan saw the second man leap at him with slashing cutlass. All Alan had time to do was shift his body so that his arm was free to raise his own cutlass. Steel clanged against steel, and the pirate fell off-balance to the stairwell. He managed to raise his weapon, but Alan's cutlass pierced his guard and drove to the hilt in the man's rib cage. When Alan withdrew it, a river of blood followed.

"Come on!" He helped Davon to her feet and they continued fighting their way toward the shuttle craft space lock.

They saw others along the way. Men raced for the stairwell from far down the corridors, and crewmen staged a brutal struggle for survival a level or two below. Swords clashed and Banning bolts cracked, the imminence of death fostering blind panic. Even Faroul was forgotten by the pirates, for dead men could not become gods. Only one objective reigned: reach the three-man shuttle and flee into space before the starship detonated into a billion chunks of metal and fiberglass.

Alan was no less desperate. He and Davon spiraled down to level two and burst into the long gray corridor that led to the shuttle lock on the right. They stepped over a dead man and waded through his blood. Three more shots rang out, and far ahead Alan could see Lindsay waging a running battle with a pirate near the space lock hatch.

Alan urged Davon on, their footsteps tolling like reverberations in a mausoleum all the way down the corridor. Just as they reached the open hatch, the sounds of battle erupted from inside and a Banning bolt whizzed by Alan's ear.

He darted back and flattened himself against the wall, pulling Davon with him.

"Behind us!" she said.

He spun to see three pirates racing toward them with drawn weapons.

"There's too many!" he exclaimed. He pivoted to the hatch, heard steel strike steel. "We've got to do it now!"

He leaped inside, and Davon went with him.

Before the sweeping glass portal at the end of the twenty-by-thirty-meter chamber lay the module, a small ship of blackened metal sitting like a bird ready for flight. A bloody hand clasped its outer latch, only to sink as the fingers carved a trail of blood down the hull. A few meters away, Lindsay struggled with a bearded pirate who suddenly disarmed him of his Banning and fell upon him with a cutlass. The blade caught his arm and Lindsay dropped to the floor, clutching a bloody elbow.

Alan ran toward them, fixing Banning sights on the pirate who was poised to thrust steel into chest.

"No!" he yelled, and the corsair turned just in time for bluish lightning to explode in his face.

Lindsay rolled away, but the shuttle caught his eye and he was on his feet, fumbling with the latch.

"They're right behind us!" Davon warned.

Alan looked back over his shoulder, anticipating the Banning bolt that would bring him down. *Got to run! Got to make it!*

Lindsay forced the shuttle open and fell inside. The hatch slammed shut like a coffin lid and Alan's blood ran cold with fear and helplessness.

"Lin!" he shouted as they reached the craft. He worked frantically with the latch, but it wouldn't give. The ship was about to explode, armed pirates were almost upon them, and they couldn't get in!

"Lindsay! It's me! Open it! You hear me? Open it, damn you!"

"They're here!" exclaimed Davon as the first of the men burst into sight.

Alan looked and saw too, but simultaneously he pounded on the hull with the cutlass hilt. "Open it!"

A Banning bolt charred the heat shields at his head even more, and he turned to find the assailant in his sights.

"Down, Davon!" he shouted, firing over her head as she flattened herself.

The corsair died in a hail of electromagnetic energy, but two more stormed into view even as he fell.

"We're pinned down!" said Alan. "Lindsay! You've got to help us!"

More Banning bolts surged past and Alan returned fire, delaying the pirates' charge only a moment. He heard metal screech behind him, and he looked back to see the hatch slide open.

"Inside!" he shouted to Davon. "I'll cover!"

He turned to fire Banning bolt after Banning bolt at the oncoming pirates. One went down to flop on the floor, and the other dropped from a wound in the leg. But a Banning was still deadly in the latter corsair's hands, and a quick bolt seared Alan's arm.

"I'm in!" cried Davon. "Now, Alan, now!"

Alan let the cutlass fall from his wounded arm and fired again, one last shot that drained his Banning, and he summoned his strength and dived through the hatch.

Davon closed it with a clang that sealed the lock. Alan scrambled over Lindsay's squirming form and seized the controls. "Grab something!" he shouted, activating the craft and sealing the space lock hatch to allow the portal to open.

Someone pounded on the outside hull, and a single scream pierced Alan to the marrow as the vacuum of space sucked the corsairs into its depths.

In another moment the main engine fired, and through the triangular portholes loomed only the blackness of the galaxy and the mysterious planet that would hold their destinies.

Chapter Twenty

The force of the engine pressed Alan back into a seat and stiffened his body. His muscles seemed bound, his face distorting uncontrollably. Then the burst of rocket fire ended and they were adrift in a sea of emptiness a thousand kilometers above a planet that had filled men with wonder ever since Kasterfayette's voyage.

In exhaustion he slumped in his seat, his hand on his brow. When he looked up, he found the wide porthole almost in his face, for this was a cramped craft with three seats and room for little else besides sophisticated instruments with multi-colored flashing lights.

A hand met his shoulder and he found Davon edging into the seat at his elbow. They stared at one another before he placed his hand on hers so that both rested on his upper arm.

He smiled, feeling a bond with her that he had never known before. "We made it," he said, barely louder than the hum of the computers. "You and me—I don't see how—but we got out together."

"I . . . I wouldn't have wanted it any other way," she whispered, and all her pent-up emotions became wetness against his nape.

He held her close, only to wince as she brushed his arm. She drew back. "You're hurt!" she exclaimed, finding the ugly burn above his elbow and the cut on his forearm.

He glanced at the wounds and shook his head. "Just barely caught me both times." He looked around at Lindsay crumpled on the floor. "Can you see how he is?"

She withdrew and Alan leaned back, feeling the pain in his arm deaden. He closed his eyes against the memories of bloodshed and burned flesh before finally opening them to the porthole. The craft had rotated, and above the pulsating curvature of the planet lay the starship, already a mere speck against a vast star cluster hundreds of thousands of light years from all he had ever known.

He clutched the arm rest. *We're out here all alone. Swallowed up in a cosmos that stretches to infinity.*

Davon touched his arm. "He's all right. The cut's not deep. I used the medical kit to bandage him. He's pretty groggy. There's a gash in his temple."

Alan kept up his stare through the porthole even as Davon eased back into her seat. He nodded to the receding ship. "That's what brought us here," he said, hearing his own words as if through a great tunnel. "That's everything we've ever been, the hatred and greed, the science we've come to worship. Everything mankind's ever been is twisted inside all of that metal. And nobody but the ones with the power can ever overcome it."

Barely discernible against a dark streak of space dust, the starship glinted like the apex of a distant peak in the last rays of day.

Mankind, reduced to a mere pinpoint.

Suddenly it exploded into sky-fire, streaking the heavens in all directions with ribbons of red, blue, orange, yellow, and then ceased to exist.

They sat stunned, a grim silence reigning over them. One moment the ship had been there, bearing any hopes they might have had of ever returning, and the next it had vanished like the ghosts of mankind's past.

"That's it," whispered Alan. He turned to Davon and took her hand: one man, one woman, their lives intertwined by fate. "There's just us, nothing else. Ever."

She trembled and he drew her close, strangely confident that everything was under control.

***

Three persons. More alone than the first shipwrecked sailors riding cresting waves in a small lifeboat. One survivor of the Alosian mines, one escapee from the Thalian brothels, and a young man, hardly more than a boy, who had masterminded it all.

Alan sat at the controls and pondered matters as night became dawn on the planet below. It didn't make sense. He glanced back at Lindsay, who still lay groggily against the rear console. How had Lin sprung him from the mines? Arranged all by himself for a pirate crew and ship to transport them to Faroul?

And the craft that had pulled into orbit directly behind them . . . If it had indeed been Poteet, what were the odds of a chance meeting in deep space? *It couldn't be.* It almost seemed as if the ship had been tailing them, and as Alan remembered the coded messages, the coldness of the vacuum outside seemed to seep into his marrow.

Mysteries. Confusion. And now, sweeping beneath, Faroul.

It had held a strange fascination for him ever since Kasterfayette had whispered of its secrets, and Davon's visions had imparted a far greater sense of awe. Now, even as the love he had discovered in the airlock waged war with his bitterness toward Poteet, something told him that those cyclonic clouds below shrouded more than the surface. They hid the very answers that had made his life different.

And with the quickness of a cutlass piercing his ribs, a long-submerged memory surfaced.

He was nine years old. He and his father sat on the rock steps of their home as insects chirped from nearby trees that stood silhouetted in the night.

"The wind," said Alan, "sometimes it feels like there's something in it touching me, making me warm."

His father placed a gentle hand his shoulder. "Don't you remember what it says in Hebrews, Alan? How He 'makes His angels winds, and His ministers a flame of fire'?"

Lines furrowed Alan's brow as he looked into the always-youthful features of his father. "But what *are* angels? You told me they were like messengers, so why can't I ever see one?"

"They're like the wind. You can feel the effects even if you don't realize they're there." He ran his fingers through the boy's hair. "And sometimes you see things right in front of you and never know it. But don't worry, Alan, you'll see them. The Bible says that 'at the end of the age the angels shall come forth.' You'll be there when it happens."

A tremble of awe passed through the boy. He turned to the tree limbs, moving in an always invisible wind, and then lifted his eyes to the starry expanse that was like a dark hood draped over him.

Only his father's voice could sweep away his qualms, redirect his gaze. "Remember Genesis six?" his father asked. "About angels marrying human women and their children growing up to be the mightiest men of old, with all kinds of power?"

Alan knitted his brow. "Did all that really happen? Could it happen again?"

His father raised his face to the sky. "See the stars, how many there are? There'll be fire, and they'll all pass away with a loud noise. The elements will dissolve and new heavens will spring into being, one with only righteousness in it. The whole universe is waiting for that fire, waiting for the day of judgment when evil will be destroyed."

He cupped his son's face in his hands and stared into his eyes. "You'll be there to see it happen, Alan."

There was even more awe in the boy now, but it was tempered with a strange confidence that everything was under control. "Will you be there too, Father? Will you still be alive when it happens?"

His father smiled. "Only men die," he said softly. Then he motioned to the sky. "Up there, far away, there was a place where all the angels lived. Then Lucifer rebelled and was cast out, and a third of the angels with him. Now, everything is perishing. But all of that's going to change. A new cosmos that won't ever die will be created. The fire's out there just waiting for the ones with the power to kindle it."

"Will it be me, Father?" asked Alan as bumps covered his spine. "Will I be the one?"

His father only smiled and tousled the boy's hair. When young Alan again lifted his gaze to the sky, the shrouding veil seemed to recede, and the twinkling of stars exploded into a raging inferno that consumed the universe. Suddenly it was as if his father stood within it, his illuminated features becoming one with the flames.

"Come, Alan," beckoned his father. "Come inside, where we have waited for you from the start of time. Come, o man of renown, come and kindle the flame of creation."

"Alan? Alan, you okay?"

Davon's voice shook him back to the here and now, but when he looked at her, he was still in awe, as if he had just beheld things man was never meant to see.

A groan rose up from behind them, and Alan turned to see Lindsay pulling himself up by the rear seat.

"Alan," he said quietly, checking the bandage on his arm. "We made it. My Lord, we *made* it."

"Yeah." Alan surveyed him up and down. "Ship blew a few minutes ago. Nobody left but us and that module from the enemy craft."

Lindsay climbed weakly into his seat and looked at Davon, who eyed him coldly. He started to speak to her, but shrugged and addressed Alan. "I . . . I was afraid the two of you wouldn't get away."

Alan studied the flashing of the console lights in Lindsay's face. "I was starting to wonder if you wanted us to."

Lindsay cleared his throat and ran his fingers nervously along the gash beside his ear. Suddenly he seemed a little boy again, wanting the man who had raised him to tell him not to worry about a misdeed.

"I-I know I . . . This knot on my head. Things are still a little fuzzy. I think I must've been out of it for a while when I first got in."

Maybe, thought Alan. Or maybe he had calculatingly denied them entry. Maybe he had been knocked silly only when G forces had slung him back upon their escape.

Seething, Alan turned back to the controls, and a grim silence ensued as the wonders of an unexplored world passed beneath.

"No starship," he finally said to Davon. "Two of them blown to pieces. And here we are clear across the galaxy in a shuttle that can't even come close to the speed of light. If I was caught up for a while in a shadow path like you say—Blake Sharrel's, Rhonda Gregory's—it looks like the one I'm on now's not going to let us go home."

Davon laid her cheek against his chest. "We never had a home back there, Alan." Then she lifted her head so that they could look in each other's eyes from centimeters away. "The only home I could ever imagine all those years was when I saw Faroul, you and me there."

Alan's chest expanded, and he looked to the porthole and the planet that filled it. "Looks like we don't have much choice anymore, do we?"

As he found her gaze yet again, he wondered if either of them had ever had another choice.

Chapter Twenty-One

Alan set the automatic pilot with the exact coordinates that Kasterfayette had whispered in his dying breaths, and on the next pass through the equatorial night the ship began its fiery descent into the atmosphere.

Sparks spawned by friction streamed upward like a thousand tiny rockets outside the portholes. The seat vibrated beneath Davon, jarring her to the bone. She clasped the arm rests and felt her heart pound like bludgeon on steel, and the flashing lights in the console became a blur and faded into esoteric memories.

She saw herself in her formative years, misunderstood, abandoned by her mother. She felt the rocks slam into her rib cage, felt the spittle run down her face. She smelled the lemstel on the breath of the man who had taken her in, turned her over to the groping hands of the bordellos. She relived the crushing of her dignity, and then *he* was there, across the smoke-infested tavern, and she had begun to live again.

He had come closer to accepting her as she was than anyone else. He had hearkened to her warning when there had been no tangible reason to. He had fought for her, lost blood for her honor, returned to her even when it had appeared she had betrayed him. She remembered his quarters in the subdued light, the touch of his embrace as he had whispered "forever."

Forever. She strained against G forces to look at him: the finely hewn chin, the eyes squeezed shut, the scars of the mines on the arms that had held her close as she had found solace at last. She wanted him forever, and yet it was as if another power called her, ruled her thoughts in wakefulness and her dreams in sleep.

Faroul. That was it, whatever it was. It was summoning her to her destiny, but what of Alan? What about their destiny together?

She wanted *him.* Nothing else.

***

The sun was a blazing sphere of blood through misty islands of blue gas when the ship began to level out in the atmosphere and the wings automatically spread. Alan glanced out the porthole at the sunrise, like fire rising out of fire, and intense *déjà vu* came over him.

This was the age of interstellar travel, when mystical fantasy and religious myth had been superseded by starships capable of traversing interstellar expanses at post-light speeds. Yet he found himself thinking of things beyond science, ideas alien to the prevailing belief in man as maker of his own fate.

Kasterfayette! He could wring that old man's neck for whispering those damnable words and setting all this in motion. It was Kasterfayette alone who had stranded Davon here, so far beyond the last outpost of hope.

Or, Alan pondered, was there another who bore just as much blame, or more? What about his own vengefulness? Would Davon have been in these straits if not for his hatred of Poteet?

But maybe something else was at play. Maybe some inexplicable force had used that very flaw in his character to lure them all to this point in space and time.

"We can't go back, can't ever go back," Lindsay mumbled from the rear seat. "The things we've always had, we can't go back, can't—"

"That's enough, Lin," said Alan.

Lindsay seized his shoulder, spinning him about. "You talked to him! Can we stay alive down there? Can—"

"Gods don't die, do they?" interrupted Alan with a glare. "Isn't that what you're planning? To be a god? You know, Lin, back when you were a kid, I caught you with my Banning down in the bay. You'd taken target practice on the booty till it was worthless. But you dropped your head and whimpered you were sorry, and all I did was put my arm around you and told you not to worry about it."

He paused, reliving the memory. "You know what I should've done? I should've taken my belt and blistered your butt till you learned right from wrong. But I didn't, and it looks like we're still paying for my mistake."

The craft sped through wispy blue clouds that hugged it and obscured all else. Abruptly they burst into daylight, and a red sea became a stunning floor a few kilometers below. It shimmered and pulsated, swirls and eddies creating maelstroms that lapped skyward in flames that changed from red to yellow to orange: a fire that seemed to burn but never consume.

Alan felt the touch of Davon's hand, and he turned to see the reflection of the sea in her eyes as she spoke.

"I . . . I've seen this all my life. I've felt it, known it, but I'm scared. I'm just so scared."

Lindsay breathed sharply. "What *is* all this crap you keep going on about? From the start you've messed things up. You've messed everything up. I tried to tell Alan not to bring you, but you had him so wrapped around your little finger he wouldn't pay any attention to a word I said. Instead of listening to anybody with any sense, all he does is listen to a bunch of nonsense from a slimy whore."

Alan whirled and seized Lindsay by the collar. "Don't you *ever* talk to her like that! You hear me? Not ever!" Shoving him into the seat, he turned back to the controls.

As the module approached a land mass, Alan took over manual operation and the wonders of the enigmatic world swept by less than a kilometer below. The sun burned through wavy clouds that sent snake-like shadows dancing across deeply etched canyons and boulder-strewn plains pockmarked by immense craters. Wind rushed across barren flats, spawning sandstorms that swirled around jagged prominences charred like heat shields. Totally without vegetation, the land held not a hint that living beings had ever trodden it.

Or had they? If there had been bleached bones and feasting vultures, Alan readily could have believed that he stared upon an immense battlefield.

He kept a close watch on the coordinates, and within minutes a vast mesa rose into bluish clouds ahead and filled the horizon. The sun carved shadows into its rough cliffs, creating an eerie pattern that eddied like the sandstorms that racked the plains.

"Up there," Alan said quietly. "Looks like that's where we're headed, what we've got waiting for us."

"I've never seen anything like it," marveled Davon.

Lindsay had slumped in his seat since his exchange with Alan, but now he straightened, his eyes growing wide.

"That's it, isn't it?" he gasped. "Faroul. My God, how I've waited to see it! We made it! We blew everybody else to hell and now we've got it all to ourselves!"

Alan breathed deeply and closed his eyes for a moment. "It means that much to you, doesn't it? It means more to you than anything."

Lindsay half-laughed. "You damned right it does. I'd climb that mountain with my bare hands if I had to, climb it and then even God wouldn't be any better. Just think, Alan. We'll be able to create anything we want! Anything!"

But Alan was lost in memory again, as though a light had flashed on, and he heard his father's smooth voice as clearly as if he stood before him.

"He was on the holy mountain of God. In the midst of the stones of fire he walked, until iniquity was found in him.

"How you are fallen from heaven, O Lucifer, son of the morning! You said in your heart, I will sit on the mountain of assembly in the far north; I will ascend above the heights of the clouds; I will make myself like the Most High!"

Suddenly Alan was afraid, because he knew they were involved in places and events totally beyond the realm of man.

Chapter Twenty-Two

Azure clouds enveloped the craft as they flew upward toward the mesa summit. Turbulence racked the craft as hail beat a staccato on the hull, and Davon was glad for the seat restraints as she peered out the porthole at her shoulder. She wiped the condensation and tried to discern the rim, but the upper slopes were hazy, as indistinct as her thoughts. She shuddered, for the visions that had bombarded her all her life were about to become reality.

Reality. What was real, and what wasn't? Her thoughts, her dreams, her desire for Alan . . . How was she to assess any of them against the starkness of a mysterious flame?

She didn't know, and yet she felt an assurance that some force had shaped the events of her life to bring her here.

***

The craft leveled out as sensors indicated they had passed above the rim, and slowly the clouds began to disperse. Within minutes they flew in sunlight, above a fog that rolled with the wind and offered fleeting glimpses of the plateau below. At times, Alan thought he could discern wispy pinnacles, ridges, gullies, as though the terrain was even more desolate and rugged than the lowlands below the mesa.

He dipped the shuttle into the fog and the craft raced onward. What was it that loomed ahead? The forms that took shape like images in broken glass, possessing at once geometric precision and disorder?

"There!" cried Davon, pressing a hand against porthole. "It almost looks like . . ."

She never finished, for as if bursting out of space dust into a star cluster, they broke into stunning daylight.

Alan started. Davon gave a short cry. Lindsay seized the back of Alan's seat.

Below, strewn like bodies in catacombs, were ruins.

Walls that had crumbled to rubble. Pockmarked pillars standing like great, fractured bones. Jagged statues pinned beneath collapsed structures. The lines, circles, and arches of once-ornate palaces, desecrated as though wrenched by stupendous forces. And an army of shattered rock, piled in massive drifts all the way to a wall of fire on the horizon.

Decadence. With the pale look of death. For everything was white with talcum-like dust that swept through cracked streets and rose in wicked whirlwinds.

"The city of Faroul!" whispered Alan.

He faced Davon, unspeakable thoughts strafing him. He turned again to the porthole, and as he sped the craft toward the red sea in the distance, his mind reeled with images of his father, the echo of his voice.

"All the angels lived there, until one day iniquity was found, and the universe began to die!"

He glanced at the console, noting the coordinates. He felt Davon's hand on his arm, and he nodded to the forward porthole. "Just a few minutes, dead ahead." Then fear gripped him.

You're out there, waiting for us. You called us across the galaxy, kept us alive. Who are you? What do you want from me? Tell me!

But the only answer was the pounding of his heart and flicker of red flames that touched the sky in the distance.

With peripheral vision, Alan saw Davon spin to the rear of the craft.

"Something's wrong!" she exclaimed. "Something's about to—"

He began to turn to her, and then a blast like a sonic boom drove him forward so that his safety belt alone saved him from the console.

"Alan!"

Her voice died in an explosive rupture of gas lines that compromised restraints, and suddenly the inside of the shuttle was a maelstrom. Alan's shoulder slammed into a porthole and his skull found the overhead instruments. He cried out, his lungs on fire from deadly gases as the craft twisted out of control.

Flames erupted in the console as instruments short-circuited. Wind roared through a hole that gaped in the hull and sucked star charts through. Alan fought against centrifugal forces that set his head swimming. The porthole before him was a blur of ruins, sky, and horizon as the ship screamed downward, tumbling crazily in the grip of physical laws that wouldn't be denied. They were mere seconds from the end, a destiny in the dust and devastation of an inexplicable world.

No! You can't have us! Not either one of us!

His fingers tightened on controls that refused to respond. He could already taste death as he anticipated the impact and conflagration. He wondered if he would feel the immense heat in his last moment, if the force would crush him before his senses could register it all.

Suddenly the frozen controls ripped free, responding at last. The ruins were a wall before him. He pulled up on the stick and the craft's nose jutted skyward. A wing clipped a pillar with a grinding *crack!*, toppling it and setting the controls to vibrating like an earthquake.

"Hold on!" he yelled, finding an ancient roadway in the porthole. "We're going down!"

The controls flew from his hands as the craft bumped the ground violently, skipped, and began to skid, twisting and grinding through a hurricane of dust. Sparks flew from friction. The hull gave way to a wrenching of metal and piercing screech. Davon cried out and clutched his arm, and then everything went still.

Dazed, Alan regained awareness to the hiss of fuel lines and billowing of dust through shattered portholes and ripped hull. Coughing, he turned for Davon and realized that her fingers were on his shoulder, gently shaking him.

"Alan . . . Alan!"

Somehow he managed a smile. "It's all right. We're here, Davon. We made it."

Then he was lost in her arms, and strangely it didn't seem to matter that they were stranded on an inhospitable world filled with mystery, and could never go back.

Never!

None of them had suffered more than minor injuries, and a few minutes later they stood outside the wrecked craft and felt the scorching sun raise beads of sweat. The wind howled through dead streets, across once-great buildings leveled as if by holocaust, and sent dust curling around pillars that stood like lonely sentinels. As Alan stirred a little, the powder crawled around his ankles and rose to choke his throat.

He looked at Lindsay, who stood beside a decadent wall.

"Well, Lindsay," he said, nodding to the shuttle wreckage. "Looks like if it was Faroul you wanted all this time, you got it. You got it and can't ever go back."

Strangely, though, the younger man seemed oblivious to Alan's pronouncement. He dropped to his knees, and the dust became like fabulous jewels running through his fingers.

"My God, we're here!" Lindsay's voice echoed as he looked up, and something maniacal filled his eyes. "I knew it. I knew I could do it. A god! You hear me? A god!"

Alan breathed sharply and looked away. When he studied the gaping hole in the craft's fuselage, he experienced an emotion as near to true hatred as he had felt since the airlock.

"Even a god has a devil to fight," he said.

"Poteet?" asked Davon.

Alan turned wary eyes on the dead city about him, and on to the sea of fire rising against the horizon. "Nobody else," he said, and the wind seemed to carry his words away, lose them in desolation. "He's waiting out there for us, Davon. He's out there, and so is something else."

When he faced her, he thought for an instant that he could see those mysterious flames alive in her eyes.

"What now?" he asked. "Stranded, no food, no water, not much chance of finding any around here. It . . . It looks like we might not make it, Davon."

She came to him, and her touch began to soothe his hopelessness. Never before had he felt such oneness with her, as if he existed only for her, and she for him.

"As long as I'm with you," she said, "even if we die, there'll be meaning to it. If we can't live together, if God doesn't intend us to, then maybe He'll let us die together."

They walked the streets of a dead city and felt intense thirst crawl down their throats. With every labored step a little cloud of white sprayed up. Leading the way toward the flaming sea, Alan climbed mounds of debris, traversed yawning abysses, skirted crumbling foundations as rubble crunched beneath his boots. The heat sapped his strength, and he looked up at the merciless sun and couldn't understand why they had been brought this far, only to die.

Halfway to the sea they stopped to hug the shade of an eroded wall. Davon's face was flushed, her breaths short, her chest heaving like bellows. With a shudder, she sank into his embrace.

"I can't, Alan . . . can't . . . make it."

Alan lifted his gaze to the razed city, and beyond to the sea that was not a sea. "You *can*, Davon. Don't you remember? You saw us there. You saw us in the heart of Faroul. You saw us and we're going there."

"And then what, Alan? There's no water, no food. Oh, Alan, then what?"

He didn't know what to tell her.

They went on, sheer determination supplanting strength. Lindsay trailed, and often Alan glanced back to see him chattering and laughing, as though he spoke to others who weren't there.

Sometimes it seemed that Alan also heard voices from the past, saw the splendor of bygone ages when a great civilization had flourished here. Who had they been? Had they merely gone away, leaving a city to fall into decadence? What about the evidence of cataclysm in these ruins, the wasteland nature of the entire world? Wasn't it as if a war beyond all wars had been waged?

Then his father's voice seemed to echo through the streets, encompassing the fallen walls and fractured pillars.

"There was war in Heaven, and the dragon and his angels were cast out!"

***

Davon, too, felt strange sensations and glimpsed visions that had haunted her all her life. She remembered the first time she had seen Alan: not in the dingy bar reeking with lemstel, but in prophecy. His had been the image of a proud, defiant man who held her in his arms before a wall of fire, held her until the flames devoured them but never destroyed.

For a moment, she shut her eyes and thanked God that Alan had taken her out of the brothels, away from the grasping arms, even if it meant she was to die in vain halfway across the galaxy.

***

The sun was sinking into the ruins to the west, casting long shadows across their path, when, near city's edge, the sea became a fiery battlement not far ahead. It rose several meters above the level of the ruins, yet remained within its own bounds, as if unseen forces held it back. Flickering tongues of red fire lapped yellow ones, and the sea's depths seemed to hold glowing gasses that pulsated, from red to orange and back again.

The sea defied scientific logic, but then what *had* followed the known laws of the universe ever since the light had appeared in Alan's cell?

Finally, long after mechanical motions had replaced conscious steps, he discerned between great mounds of debris the scene that he had sought since the crash: a beach with crumbling wall that fronted the ocean as far as he could see. He went closer, and the change in perspective allowed a look through a great arched gate that framed the boiling flames.

"That's it," Alan whispered, remembering Kasterfayette's description. "My Lord, it's Faroul."

He was there. Nine and a half years after a dying old man had whispered secrets, he was there. And still he didn't know what to believe.

"I lost it, and I can never have it again!"

Kasterfayette's words seemed to rise to a crescendo that forced him to cover his ears. Then a hand was on his shoulder, and Davon's voice swept aside the haunting words.

"Alan? What is it? What's wrong?"

"Kasterfayette," he said, feeling a cold sweat. "If he couldn't have it, then what are *we* doing here? My Lord, Davon, I never believed a word of it. If I had, do you think I would've ended up on Alos? Don't you think I would've done everything I could to get here?"

He looked beyond her at Lindsay, who stood strangely attentive for the first time in a long while. "It's all your doing, Lindsay, damn you! Why'd you have to come after me? Look at all this. You think if a person could get the power to create, everybody here would've vanished without a trace? There's *not* any power of creation. There never was, not for Kasterfayette, not for Poteet, not for you or anybody else but the ones with power already. You hear me? You're going to die here!"

Once more, Davon's touch calmed his nerves.

"It was never an accident we met, Alan Burke," she whispered. "If it all ends right here, I'll still believe God brought you and me together. My whole life, I've prayed for somebody. I couldn't understand why it was *me* that was different, couldn't ever be accepted. Then one night I saw somebody across a bar, and it was like I'd always known he would be there, that he'd become part of my life. I'm not sorry we ended up here, Alan, because I love you."

She kissed him, and he was not sorry either that he had heeded her warning that night in a palace of delights so many thousands of light years away.

Chapter Twenty-Three

As they skirted an imploded structure at city's edge, Alan stumbled and reached for a remnant of wall. The instant he gripped a protruding block, it burst in his hand and shrapnel flew. He pivoted, the report of a Banning in his ears.

"Watch out!" he yelled, dragging Davon down with him.

Lindsay froze, and then a second bolt sprayed him with gravel and he dropped to the ground. Legs squirming, he clawed at the rubble, but a third shot reverberated through the ruins before he gained cover beside Davon.

As Alan checked, he found the rising dust still crackling with electromagnetic energy.

"Poteet!" exclaimed Davon.

Alan felt blood trickle from a cut in his brow. "He's not giving up Faroul to anybody!"

"We're pinned down!" said Lindsay. "My God, do something!"

Alan looked about, trying to locate the source of the Banning fire: somewhere high and across the avenue ahead, he judged, eighty or ninety meters away. Surveying a hill of debris that rose fifty meters against the sinking sun, he tried to discern the shadows within shadows. Suddenly, blue lightning flared from a murky point near the summit.

Rubble detonated in his face and he threw an arm about Davon. "We've got to get out of here! He'll change his position, pick us off!"

"Do something!" Lindsay kept muttering. "He's going to blow the hell out of us!"

Alan shifted just enough to note the lay of the avenue back toward the city's heart. Immediately behind them lay a ten-meter exposed stretch, then a meter-high foundation that cut across the avenue at a ninety-degree angle.

"The low wall," he said. "When I draw his fire, run for it!"

"You'll be killed!" argued Davon.

"Run!"

Scrambling to his feet, Alan stumbled over rocks into the line of fire.

"Poteet!" he shouted.

Even as Alan dodged, a Banning bolt seared past his skull and raised the hairs on his tingling scalp. He remained a swerving target as Davon and Lindsay ran for the foundation, and he dived away just in time to avoid a shot that split a boulder at his knee.

He rolled into the clearing and the dust powdered up. Then he was on his feet, all senses fixed on that low foundation that seemed so close, yet so far. He could almost feel a Banning bolt between his shoulders and taste his own charred flesh. A shot struck the ground at his heels, and then another exploded against the foundation as he fell over it.

Momentarily protected, he found Davon at his side and Lindsay in a fetal position beyond.

"He'll be coming after us!" Alan warned.

"He keeps shooting and shooting!" muttered Lindsay. "Doesn't he know—"

"We can't just lay here and wait," said Alan. "I'm going after him."

Davon clutched his shoulder. "He'll kill you. You can't. Alan, you can't!"

He turned to find her chin quaking. "He comes off that hill, we're dead anyway."

Her arms went about him and she clung tightly as if she never intended to let go. "Don't leave me. If we're going to die . . . Please don't go off!"

Alan disengaged her arms. "I've got to. If I don't make it . . ."

She reached for him again, but he belly-crawled away through the shadows of the foundation.

***

Alan's boots dug into debris and slid as it gave. He clutched jagged edges of hewn stones that abraded his hands. He went on all fours, or in a crawl that raised blood in his trousers knees. And through every centimeter of the climb, he searched for the crest of the long ridge that stood against the fading day.

You're up there, Poteet. I know you're up there, waiting to kill us. Come on then, you swine. Let's do it.

The sky drew nearer, until it seemed only meters away. A megalith rose up over Alan, and as he reached to dig fingernails into a fracture, rubble tumbled from the top.

He froze. The gravel pelted him and rolled on down the hill with an almost musical tone. Quietly he withdrew his hand from the fracture and reached for a skull-sized rock at his hip. He heard the crunch of boots: one step, then another, as they neared the edge. He could almost feel the presence of that unseen person, here in the city of the dead, and he tightened his grip on the stone.

Just a little farther. Just one more step.

A boot jutted over the ledge, then leg, arm, shoulders—and a man became silhouetted against the sky.

Now!

The rock in his hand became raw power that exploded with a primal yell and the snap of elbow and wrist. The recoil threw Alan off-balance and he tumbled back, flailing for support. Even so, he heard the rock thud home against stomach and bone to a loud *oomph*!

He looked up to see the silhouette double over, clutch abdomen, sink to knees. Then Alan was scrambling up the boulder, lunging and seizing the legs, his attention fixed on the Banning in the man's grip. But the moaning figure shook Alan free and a boot heel caught him in the face.

The Banning! Got to get up, stop him!

He clutched the wrist above the weapon, only to meet a flashing fist that set the world spinning darkly, shadows swirling through shadows. He was like a boxer ruled only by the instinct to dodge the next blow and the one after that. But there was something more, as if unearthly power pierced his cells and left them shrieking a single word that seemed to exist only for him, and he for it.

Faroul!

The two fell along the crest, a tangle of arms and legs against the swollen orb of orange that sank into the sea. Blood splattered as fists flew, and then Alan stunned him with an elbow to the ear. Coming to a knee as the man collapsed, Alan seized a rock and yanked the tangled beard so that they were face to face.

He looked at the scar creasing the beard at the jaw, the close-set eyes, the Indian-like cheekbones, the black mole on his nose.

"Look at me!" he cried. "Look at me and die, you son of a bitch!"

Drawing back his arm, he readied to crush the skull, only to hesitate as if an unseen force stayed his arm.

Here was his second in command, the traitor who had stood laughing as U.S.S. guards had dragged Alan away to die in hell. Here was the animal who had fomented such hatred in him, the one whose anticipated death had ruled him for nine years.

But other memories deluged him as well, visions of a being of light who had swept away the vengeance and changed him. In his presence, Alan had felt alive, truly *alive*, for the first time. Even now, he would have given anything in the universe just to have bathed in his warmth again, basked in his infinite love.

Alan tossed the rock aside and found the Banning nearby. "Get up," he ordered, pulling at the beard.

The man groaned and Alan stepped back, watching with leveled Banning as his enemy came to an elbow, then a knee. The dark eyes looked up through blood and sweat, and Alan peered into the soul of a devil.

"Been a long time, hasn't it, Poteet? Guess it's a small galaxy after all."

"Why don't you kill me?" Poteet asked, touching the cut on his lip with the back of his hand.

"I died for nine years. Maybe something quick's too good for you. Now get up!"

Chapter Twenty-Four

From beyond the foundation, Davon heard boots sliding down the slope, crushing rocks and creating small landslides near the sea of fire.

Her pulse raced. *Don't let him be dead! Don't let him die without me!*

A voice sounded, too far away to distinguish. She froze, not even breathing as she listened, but all was silent now except for the crunching of debris.

A word wavered on her lips, one that had become as much a part of her as her own heart. She shuddered, anticipating that it might be someone else, that he lay dead in a pool of blood.

No!

The voice sounded again, this time distinctly, and the word burst from her lungs.

"Alan!"

Jumping to her feet, she scrambled over the foundation and sprinted toward the wall of fire. On the hillside ahead she saw the man she loved escorting another, their forms like wraiths against the glowing sea. She met them at the base, emotion overwhelming her.

Alan smiled. "Made it." Then his voice choked a little. "I don't know what happens from here on, Davon. But we'll face it together. I promise you."

The man who must have been Poteet spat between leche-stained teeth, the spittle clinging to a rock. His bloody face was bathed in eerie light from the sea as he stared at the Banning muzzle before his chest.

Alan's finger twitched on the pressure release as he nodded to the pirate. "Want you to meet an old friend," he said sarcastically. "Meet my second-in-command, the filthy dog that sold me out."

Poteet's puffed upper lip jerked nervously. "You had to have Faroul all to yourself, didn't you, Burke. Nine and a half years ago we could've worked together, shared it all. But you didn't want it that way." He rubbed his nose into his shoulder and spat again. "You didn't want anybody else to have it, even know about. That's why I sold you out, you greedy bastard."

"*You* couldn't ever have it anyway, Poteet. You think you can. Everybody this side of hell thinks they can." He nodded to the flames. "Look at it! Look! Because you'll never have it! Not you or anybody else!"

Lindsay came struggling up over debris in the avenue and stopped at Davon's shoulder. Alan motioned to him.

"You remember Lindsay, don't you, Poteet? The skinny little boy who was always asking you questions, the kid you sent off to die in prison?" Alan's fingers tightened on the Banning. "Kind of reminds you of old times, doesn't it, the three of us together. Seems like I remember a filthy swine standing and laughing as a dozen guards dragged Lin and me away."

Poteet grinned. "One of my favorite memories." He surveyed Lindsay: the blood on his upper arm, the heaving chest, the shiver that swept through his frame, the lips straining to form words that wouldn't come.

The pirate looked back at Alan and smiled smugly. "You should've seen your face that night when those guards poured in, didn't even touch me. You just couldn't bear to think somebody had outsmarted you, that you could've misjudged somebody so much." He gave a half-laugh. "Don't guess you've ever made that mistake again, have you?"

"You talk big for a man about to go to hell," said Alan. "You know, Poteet, there's a few things about all this I can't quite figure out, some things that just don't click. If you knew how to get here, if you heard over the intercom what Kasterfayette told me, why wait nine years?

And it seems awfully peculiar that you happened to pop up just when we got into orbit, almost like you'd been waiting for us. Or following."

Poteet looked down and laughed. "Now what makes you think that?" He rubbed his shin where blood seeped through his trousers. "Well, I'll tell you, Burke. Sometimes it all comes down to who you can trust and who you can't."

Davon realized too late what was happening. The clue lay in Poteet's fingers: a twitch, a sudden jerk, a quick downward movement. She wanted Alan to fire the Banning, but it all happened too fast. The pirate's hand scraped the ground and scooped dust that flew out, a sandstorm that filled Alan's eyes.

Davon cried out and Poteet was upon him, wrestling for the Banning, sinking a knee into his midriff. Alan fell back, dragging the pirate with him, and the weapon clanged to the ground. As they struggled fiercely beside it, Davon spun to Lindsay.

"Do something! Do something, Lindsay!"

But Lindsay hesitated, and when she bolted for the Banning herself, she tripped and went down hard. With barely a pause, she lunged for the weapon, only to see a hand take it up just before she could reach it.

Lindsay stood, the Banning in his grip and the flaming sea in his eyes. When he squeezed the pressure release, lightning cracked and disintegrated a rock beside the men.

***

The blast was stunning, more so for Poteet than for Alan, who came to his knee and seized the groggy pirate by the collar.

"I should've killed you when I had the chance. Now get up!"

When Alan looked at Lindsay three paces away, the Banning loose at his side, he smiled at the younger man.

"Looks like I owe you another one. I'm glad you were here, Lin, glad you're on my side." He looked down to gain the support of a small boulder and struggled up. "You know Lin, I—"

Facing Lindsay, Alan couldn't believe what he saw.

Lindsay had leveled the Banning on Alan.

"You bastard!" cried Davon, seizing a rock from where she knelt.

Lindsay swung the weapon toward her. "Drop it! Or I'll get rid of you once and for all!"

As Davon complied, Lindsay withdrew until he could cover them both. Meanwhile, Poteet gained his feet and grinned.

"Why, Lin?" asked Alan. Memories of a boy for whom he would have done anything flashed through his mind. "Is it something I did? Something I didn't do for you?"

Poteet went to Lindsay and took the weapon. The pirate laughed and blood trickled from his lip, becoming lost in his beard. "Well, well," he told Alan caustically, "looks like you still don't know who to trust, do you?"

Alan stared at Lindsay and then hung his head. He looked up only when he felt Davon's hands on his upper arm. Somehow, he had never felt closer to her.

"Davon." The very sound of her name solaced him. "I wanted us to be together, to live together forever. At least—oh, Davon! Now we can die together, can't we?"

She looked at him, seemingly unable to find words of her own, but he knew it was the end that she would have chosen.

Poteet spat between his teeth. "Very touching." He nodded to Davon. "She must be the whore that messed everything up."

Alan looked at Lindsay, who stood with lowered head, his entire frame on the verge of sinking. "You haven't told me why, Lin. Can't you even look at me and tell me? Don't you owe me that much?"

Lindsay kept his gaze to the ground as he turned and slunk away.

Poteet wiped the blood under his nose. "Well, if *he* won't tell you, I will. You thought you gave that boy everything, but you didn't. You wouldn't let him have the greatest thing of all. You wouldn't let *any* of us have it. You were a fool, Burke. Didn't you think we'd find some way to get it?

"After I sold you out to the government, got a pardon, I tried for the longest to figure out a way to get here. Problem was, you were the only one that knew how. It took me nine years, but finally I got a plan in my head. I checked on you, found out you were still alive, then I put some credits in the right hands, got Lindsay freed from prison. And believe me, by that time he *wanted* Faroul. He wanted the power of creation so bad it almost busted his guts.

"I made a few more bribes, got him on as a guard. I got to hand it to the wimp, he did what he was supposed to. Even so, there was still a problem. We knew you'd never tell anybody where Faroul was, not even him, and that something out here would have to be pretty attractive to lure you."

Poteet laughed. "Like my neck."

He spat again. "I had a deal with Juarez. You'd guide them to Faroul and I'd be on your butts, and when we got here we'd rendezvous, kill you and split everything. But you had to go and mess things up, didn't you? You had to go and kill Juarez, leave it up to Lindsay to key me in on what was happening.

"But I'm here now, damn you, no matter how much you didn't want anybody else to have it."

Alan nodded to the sea of fire. "There it is. Faroul, the gate. So why the hell don't you just go out in it? Go! Take it, you pig! Take it all if you think you can!"

Poteet glanced at it before rubbing his nose and grinning. "First things first," he said, his fingers tightening on the Banning. He surveyed them coldly and Alan's arm went about Davon, accepting her head against his heart.

Alan closed his eyes, thanking the being of light for bringing Davon into his life, even if only for the purpose of dying in each other's arms. Somehow it almost seemed right to him, as if they had lived all their lives, suffered through all that they had, just to be together in death, here across the galaxy, a man and a woman before a flaming sea.

"But you know something, Burke?"

Alan opened his eyes to see Poteet framed against the gate to Faroul. The pirate nodded toward it with the Banning. "Why should I kill you with this little toy when I can destroy you as a god? I want to see your eyes when I come out of Faroul, when I kill you just by willing it."

His gaze shifted to Davon, and there was something in his expression that made her cling even more tightly to Alan.

"As for you, well, uh . . ." Poteet grinned and looked her up and down, the full breasts, slim waist, curved hips. He laughed, revealing broken teeth. "Even a god needs a woman. But seems to me that's *all* I need. I sure don't need a whimpering little swine at my side."

He turned and leveled the Banning on Lindsay.

"No!" yelled Alan.

Lightning blitzed, an azure bolt of energy streaming outward. It detonated against Lindsay's back, slamming him into a crumbling wall where his face smeared a bloody trail down to the dust.

Poteet pivoted back to Alan. "You're next! The hand of God himself is going to blow you to hell!"

He turned and ran toward the sea of fire, where the arched gate yawned wide like an abyss.

Chapter Twenty-Five

Davon squeezed Alan's hand, and the touch calmed his shudder. They watched Poteet recede toward the sea, and then Alan turned to the body crumpled at the base of blood-streaked ruins.

"Lindsay," he said quietly.

A grim silence ruled as they went hand-in-hand across the avenue to the scene. The young man lay face down, arms extended, his blood still trickling down the wall at his fingertips. The stench of burned flesh hung over him. Alan knelt, and when he ran his hand underneath to turn Lindsay, he could feel exposed intestines hot against his palm.

Alan rolled him over and an eyelid quivered. The lips began to move, and Alan put his arm under Lindsay's shoulder and supported his head.

"Oh, Lin!" said Alan. "I tried to give you everything, tried to be like a father!"

The young man coughed, spraying Alan's shirt with specks of blood. Lindsay reached for him, his fingers closing on his arm, wrenching it as though it was the only thing to hold on to in life. Faintly, through horrible coughs that shook his body, two words sank deep into Alan's fiber. *"I'm . . . sorry!"*

All his life, desire for revenge had dominated Alan. From the moment he had held the dead falcon, he had sworn vengeance on anyone who did him wrong. He had never been able to overlook betrayal, as though it were a cancer that ate away at him, gave him no rest, no peace, until it was avenged.

God! How he had hated anyone who had plotted against him, done something behind his back! He had wanted nothing but to bury his fingers in their throats and send them to hell!

Then the being of light had come and filled him with other things, nobler ideas. Now, the boy he had loved as a son, the one who had been his sole link to anything kind and gentle for long years on a pirate ship, lay dying.

Dying after betraying him.

Alan took him in his arms, looking at the face, remembering him as a boy, the wide eyes, broad smile, cheerful voice. He held him close and for the first time in his life whispered three words.

"I forgive you. I forgive you, Lin."

Lindsay's eyes rolled up into their sockets and he convulsed and grew still, his head in final repose on Alan's arm.

Alan closed his eyes against a sudden mist, and the touch of Davon's hand brought him comfort.

"I'm sorry, Alan," she said softly as he stood. "I never realized how much he meant to you, how much you loved him."

Alan looked one last time into the lifeless face. "I never realized it either," he said hoarsely.

He turned and walked away a few steps, shaking himself like a boxer clearing his head after a knockdown. Davon came to his side, and together they gazed at the sea, where a silhouette was framed by the arch in the wall. The flames distorted the image like wispy waves of heat rising from a campfire, until the figure became lost inside the whirlpool of lapping orange and red tongues.

"I could have killed Poteet," said Alan, staring until all was a blur. "I could have split his skull with a rock, opened his heart with a Banning. But I couldn't bring myself to." He turned to her, revealing with a look the things he couldn't voice.

"Are you sorry you didn't?" she asked.

"That's just it. It's as if I've changed. I don't want to hurt anybody anymore. It doesn't matter what anybody's done to me. Just like with

Lin, after all he'd done. I really meant it when I told him I forgave him. It's as if there's just love and nothing else. No other reason for living, no other purpose for being here in Faroul."

"I'm glad, Alan, I'm glad all the hatred's gone, glad there's something else inside you."

"There's another thing I need to get squared," he said. "It's you. When you told me Juarez forced himself on you, I tried to put it out of my mind, forget it. But I never forgave you because I didn't believe you. But now there's not even any question in my mind, I'm so sure of what you told me." He lowered his head. "Now if you can only forgive *me*."

Her arms went about his neck, and he looked up to see her smiling. "You don't even have to ask."

She withdrew abruptly. "Poteet. He'll be coming back after us. We've got to get out of here."

Alan shook his head. "Kasterfayette. *He* couldn't keep it. Poteet can't either."

"But the power of creation. Is it real, Alan? Are you sure it's something he can't have?"

Her eyes went glassy as though a fog swept over them. She seized Alan's arm, lines creasing her face as if she saw things that weren't there, heard words that had not been voiced.

"Davon?"

She began to swoon and he took her by the shoulders. "Davon! What's wrong? What is it you see?"

She opened her eyes, and they were like those of one who has witnessed places and events not lawful to reveal. She looked toward the ocean of fire almost longingly, and then back at Alan.

"It . . . It's like I suddenly understand it all," she gasped. "Like for the first time in my life it makes sense. The gate, the fire, Faroul! In

Heaven's name, Alan, it's waiting there for us. It's always been waiting for us!"

She nodded to the fires. "Let's go to it. Let's go inside, Alan, and together we'll find things nobody else has ever known."

He drew back, fear shrouding him, fear of what he couldn't understand, fear of the abrupt change in her.

A loud cry startled him. It echoed from boulders and pillars, rocked the city of the dead, and he spun to see Poteet walk out of the sea of fire.

He was a man, but something beyond sinew and bones. It was as if Alan saw him through a glass that warped Poteet's image, distorting it into a wispy figure glowing scarlet and orange, with flames dancing between his splayed fingers, and eyes that blazed like white-hot coals.

"Look!" screamed Poteet, the words casting a chill in the air. "Look at your god!"

He raised a fiery hand.

"Watch out!" Alan gave warning and pulled Davon down with him.

Lightning surged overhead and exploded against a pillar, felling it with a roar and strafing the area with rock. Throwing a protecting arm over Davon, Alan realized with a start that the bolt *had not come from a Banning*.

A maniacal laugh reverberated through the relics, quaking rubble and sending small landslides down hills of debris. Alan's arm remained across Davon as they huddled in the rocks, and he felt her fighting his grip as if she wanted to rise.

"Stay down!" he pleaded.

"No," she said calmly. "I *know*, Alan. Trust me, I just *know*. We don't have to run, not from him or anybody else, not anymore."

She slipped from his grasp and stood, an unwavering profile flickering in the light of the ocean.

From eighty yards distant across the beach, Poteet came toward them. "Look at me!" he yelled. "Are you ready for a god, you whore?"

Davon stared at him as though there was nothing else in the galaxy, and then her hand came down and found Alan's. There was something in the touch that told him not to be afraid, that all was happening as it was supposed to, that everything was beyond his control, as his whole life had been.

He rose and faced the eerie, glowing figure that stood against the battlement of fire that flared in the dusk.

Poteet laughed. The walls shook. The entire mesa seemed to growl. And the sea of fire grew brighter.

"You could have had it, Burke!" he shouted with hollow voice. "We could have shared it! We could have shared it forever!"

"I thought there could only be one god," replied Alan. "And one devil."

"Die, you bastard!" screamed Poteet, lifting a hand toward him. "Die by the power you wanted all for yourself!"

A strange sensation surged through Alan, like that he had known beneath the Rayolian Crystal and atop the ridge of debris. Everything in his experience told him to dive away, to seize Davon's arm and run for cover. But something else was inside him now, something that defied logic, transcended his senses.

In that instant, he squeezed Davon's hand, and his tingling fingers twitched as if an electrical current surged from her body into his, and back again.

A fiery bolt of lightning streaked toward them from Poteet's outstretched hand, illuminating the ruins with ineffable brilliance. There was a sudden snapping, an abrupt click in Alan's mind, a spasm in Davon's hand and his, and the lightning seemed to slow. Bend. Fold backward, a jagged ray of awesome energy that raced toward the sea and exploded against the god who had hurled it.

Upheaval shook the ruins, toppling pillars, crashing boulders from the heights. A shock wave threw Alan backward with Davon, the brightness leaving specks dancing before his eyes.

For long seconds he lay beside her in the dirt, confusion reigning, inexplicable enigmas bathing his forehead with cold sweat. Edging to his elbow, he reached for her, and together they rose to look toward the shadowy beach.

And saw only the summoning flames of Faroul.

Alan closed his eyes, Kasterfayette's words dominating his thoughts. *"To the ones with the power goes the secret of creation!"*

Alan looked at Davon with awe.

"It's you," he whispered. "It's you that has the power, the one that got me out of Alos, wielded that cutlass to save me in the airlock."

"No," she said. "It's us."

Together they negotiated the boulder-strewn avenue and crossed the sandy beach. Alan's boot kicked something on the ground, and he stopped to see Poteet's Banning at his feet. He knelt and clasped it, but somehow it seemed foreign, as though it didn't belong in his fingers, his entire being rebelling at the touch.

They went on until the decaying wall closed in, the eroded arch of the gate shading them from the glare of the ocean. Alan hesitated, the hewn blocks of stone looming above. Cracked and pockmarked, they bore weather-beaten inscriptions.

Alan went nearer, straining to discern them. Then it burst upon him, setting him trembling, an iciness covering him despite the flames.

"What is it?" asked Davon. "You understand it, know what it means, don't you?"

"It's Hebrew, like Kasterfayette said." His voice was quiet, reverent. "'Mighty ones, fathered by sons of God . . .'" He whirled to her. "Davon! It says they'll walk in the fire, kindle the flames of creation, bring new heavens and Earth into existence."

"Alan!" She seized his arm and pointed. "Look! Inside the ocean! For God's sake, do you see?"

Alan looked and there seemed to be a multitude of beings within: wispy wavy figures, not men, but something else, something beyond. He drew back, shuddering, for there was something familiar about one of them, something that pricked his memory, his very essence. Yes, it was in the eyes, the hair, the glow that encompassed the face.

His father! In Heaven's name, it looked like his father!

The figure stood in the edge of the flames, beckoning, and then Alan remembered his father's words so clearly that he didn't know but that he heard them now.

"Come, Alan. Come inside, where we have waited for you from the start of time. Come, o man of renown, come and kindle the flame of creation!"

Somehow Alan seemed to know that the transfigured forms of Blake Sharrel, whose shadow path he had followed, and of Rhonda Gregory, whose wake had swept Davon up, also walked that sea. Then, as if from an infinitely small speck deep in the fire, the being of light came swiftly, the flames rolling back in his wake.

He grew in size until all else was obliterated, and he was before Alan as a man crucified, as scintillating as a billion suns, a billion galaxies. His radiance flooded Alan's eyes, filled his senses with warmth and strength. An overwhelming sensation of love enveloped him like a hen hovering over her chicks, driving out all else except the desire to be with him, to bathe in his glorious love, to be in communion with him forever.

Alan reached for Davon's hand and she turned to him, the answers to her lifetime of mystery unfolding in her face like a banner in the heavens.

He squeezed her fingers. "Poteet's shuttle," he said quietly. "It's around here somewhere. We could find it, find some place on this planet where we could live."

"Is that what you want?" she asked.

"I . . . I don't know."

"Then come with me!" she whispered. "Don't you see this is how it's supposed to be, Alan? Come with me inside Faroul!"

He stiffened and withdrew a step, memories of all he had ever known deluging him. The Banning became heavy in his hand, and he glanced down at it, noting the scratches in the grip, the reflections that played along the barrel. Somehow it seemed his only link with the past, with a life as far removed in time and space as eternity itself.

"It's the way I've always seen it," said Davon, her face bright as a sunrise. "Us, together, the way it was intended from the dawn of life." She tugged at his arm. "Come, Alan Burke, and together we'll help recreate worlds, throw out everything that's evil, create a new universe that won't ever die. Just like us."

He looked into her eyes and saw the reflection of the being of light and the flames that burned but never consumed. The Banning grew loose in his fingers and dropped to the ground. The wind howled and swept sand across the beach, eddying about it, burying it to be melted like all the elements of the cosmos.

Alan smiled and pulled her close, overcome by a tranquility that was beyond description. He kissed her tenderly, a kiss filled with more love than he had ever thought himself capable of feeling.

"I've always known I should have a destiny, Davon," he said as his eyes welled. "I've always known I should have, but never thought I would."

He took her hand, and together they walked toward the flames of Faroul.

THE END

About the Author

The author of twenty-seven books, including *Starflight to Destiny*, Patrick Dearen is a 2022 Texas Literary Hall of Fame inductee. As a nonfiction writer, he has produced books such as *A Cowboy of the Pecos*; *Saddling Up Anyway: The Dangerous Lives of Old-Time Cowboys*; and *Castle Gap and the Pecos Frontier, Revisited*. His novel *The Big Drift* received the Spur Award of Western Writers of America and the Peacemaker Award of Western Fictioneers. His other western-themed novels include *When Cowboys Die* (a Spur Award finalist), *Grizzly Moon, The End of Nowhere, Haunted Border, The Illegal Man, To Hell or the Pecos, Perseverance, Apache Lament*, and *Dead Man's Boot*.

A ragtime pianist and wilderness enthusiast, Dearen lives with his wife in Texas. See patrickdearen.com for more information.

Now Available!

SPUR AWARD-WINNING AUTHOR
PATRICK DEAREN

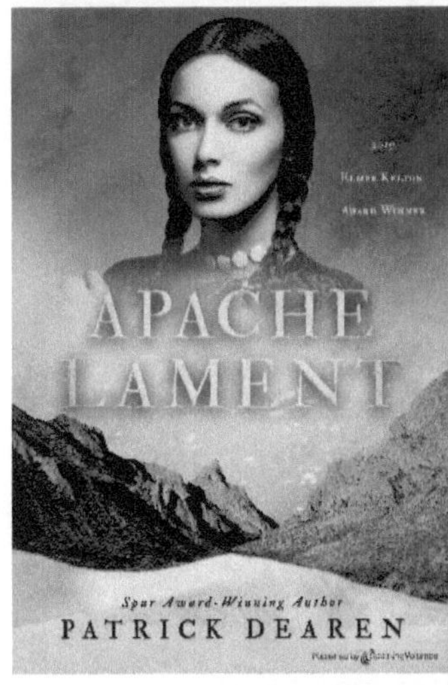
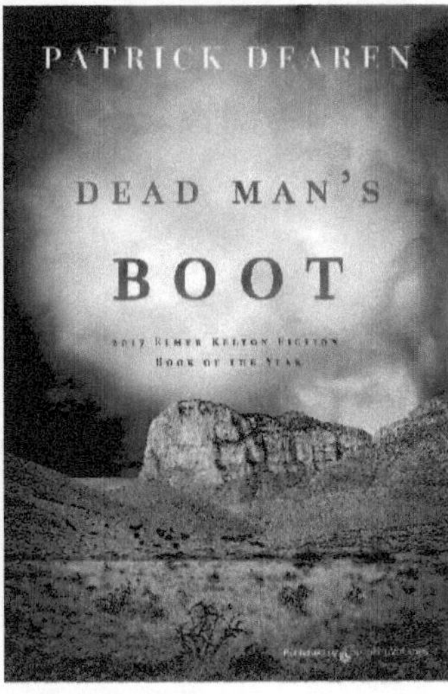

**For more information
visit: www.SpeakingVolumes.us**

Now Available!

P.M. GRIFFIN

Excellent Science Fiction Adventures

**For more information
visit: www.SpeakingVolumes.us**

www.ingramcontent.com/pod-product-compliance
Lightning Source LLC
Chambersburg PA
CBHW060536160726
47991CB00001B/350